purposeful Science

Level Three

student booklets

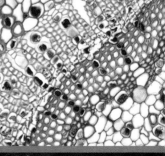

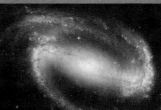

Purposeful Design Publications is the publishing division of the Association of Christian Schools International (ACSI) and is committed to the ministry of Christian school education, to enable Christian educators and schools worldwide to effectively prepare students for life. As the publisher of textbooks, trade books, and other educational resources within ACSI, Purposeful Design Publications strives to produce biblically sound materials that reflect Christian scholarship and stewardship and that address the identified needs of Christian schools around the world.

References to books, computer software, and other ancillary resources in this series are not endorsements by ACSI. These materials were selected to provide teachers with additional resources appropriate to the concepts being taught and to promote student understanding and enjoyment.

Unless otherwise identified, all Scripture quotations are taken from the Holy Bible, NEW INTERNATIONAL VERSION® (NIV®), © 1973, 1978, 1984 by International Bible Society. All rights reserved worldwide.

Photographs of pine, oleander, and hemlock plant cells in Lesson 2.3 used by permission of the Brightfield Microscopy Digital Image Gallery and Florida State University.

Photograph of Alice Eastwood in Lesson 3.1 used by permission of the California Academy of Sciences. Photo by G. A. Eisen taken either in 1909 or 1912.

Drawings of stems and roots in Lesson 3.2 used by permission of Colorado State University Cooperative Extension: www.ext.colostate.edu. From Plant Structures: Stems, Fact Sheet 7.704 and Roots, Fact Sheet 7.703.

Pictures of carnival rides used in Lesson 5.2 used by permission of Six Flags Elitch Gardens, Denver, CO.

Picture of MyPyramid used in Lesson 10.4 used by permission of Center for Nutrition Policy and Promotion, USDA.

Photograph of Mystic Falls, William Henry Jackson Collection, CHS.J705 in Lesson 13.1 used by permission of the Colorado Historical Society.

"Now" photograph in Lesson 13.1 used by permission of JohnFiedler.com. From the book Colorado 1870–2000.

Photograph of seismograph used in Lesson 13.6 used by permission of Tom Pfeiffer: www.decadevolcano.net.

Photograph of Mount St. Helens in Lesson 13.6 used by permission of USDA Forest Service, Mount St. Helens National Volcanic Monument.

Photograph of a surface rupture along a fault line in California near Hector Mine in Lesson 13.7 used by permission of Chris Wells, Earth Consultants International.

Photograph of Henrietta Swan Leavitt in Lesson 15.1 used by permission of the American Association of Variable Star Observers (AAVSO), Cambridge, MA.

Photograph of the Big Dipper in Lesson 15.5 used by permission of Till Credner: AlltheSky.com/.

Mentos® is a trademark of the Van Melle Company, which does not sponsor, authorize, or endorse this textbook.

STYROFOAM® is a trademark of the Dow Chemical Company, which does not sponsor, authorize, or endorse this textbook.

Printed in the United States of America
16 15 14 13 12 11 10 09   4 5 6 7

Purposeful design science, level three
Purposeful Design Science series
ISBN 978-1-58331-207-0   Student edition   Catalog #7507

Purposeful Design Publications
A Division of ACSI
PO Box 65130 • Colorado Springs, CO 80962-5130
Customer Service: 800-367-0798 • www.acsi.org

purposeful design
Science
Level Three

Executive Editor
Derek Keenan, Ed.D.

Editorial Director
Steven Babbitt

Managing Editor
John Conaway

Editing Team
Bonnie Church
David Hill
Stephen Johnson
Vanessa Rough
Kara Underwood

Design Team
Susanna Garmany
Sarah Schultz
Chris Tschamler

student
booklets

purposeful design
p u b l i c a t i o n s
A Division of ACSI
Colorado Springs, Colorado

purposeful design
Science

Purposeful Design Publications is deeply grateful to the faculty and staff of Briarwood Christian School in Birmingham, Alabama, for the valuable and insightful contributions they have made to the structure and content of the Purposeful Design Science series.

Table of Contents

Finding Answers to Science Questions

When scientists want to solve problems or answer questions about the natural world, they use the scientific method. To use the scientific method, follow these steps:

1. State the problem.

What question do you want to answer?

"Which cup will keep liquid hot longer?"

2. Form a hypothesis.

A hypothesis is a prediction or statement that can be tested to tell whether it is true. What do I think is the answer to my question?

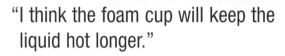

"I think the foam cup will keep the liquid hot longer."

3. Plan a way to test the hypothesis.

What experiment will show whether my prediction is correct?

4. Test the hypothesis.

Do the experiment.

5. Collect and analyze the data.

Record the results of the experiment.
Organize the information.

	Initial temperature	Temperature after 10 minutes	Temperature after 20 minutes	Temperature after 30 minutes
Foam cup	65° C			
Ceramic mug	65° C			

6. Draw conclusions and communicate results.

Was my hypothesis correct?
Has my question been
answered? Do I need to do
another experiment? How can
I show the results of my
experiment?

"My hypothesis was correct."

My Booklet about Ecosystems

Name _____

adaptation	hibernate
camouflage	migrate
compete	niche
consumer	organism
decomposer	perish
ecologist	predator
ecology	prey
ecosystem	producer
environment	relocate
food chain	scavenger
food web	

What lives in your environment?

Think about all the things plants and animals need to survive. All living things need air, food, water, and shelter. An organism is a living thing. Is a plant an organism? Is a fly an organism?

All organisms need a place to live. Everything around an organism is its environment. In an environment, an organism finds everything it needs to live including air, food, water, and shelter. An environment includes living and nonliving things. Nonliving things include rocks, minerals, air, and water.

An ecosystem consists of a group of living and nonliving things that interact with each other in an environment. How do plants and animals use nonliving things in their environment? How can a rock be helpful to a plant or animal? God has given us the responsibility for the other living things on this earth. In order to do this job, we need to learn all we can about how plants and animals live.

The scientific study of the relationship between living things and their environment is called ecology. Ecology is important because it helps us identify problems within our environment. A scientist who studies the relationship between living things and their environment is called an ecologist.

A heron can find food, water, shelter, and air in this wetland environment. ▼

A Famous Ecologist

At an early age, Rachel Carson was curious about animals. She would study and read to find out more about animals. As she grew older, she attended college to become a writer. She never forgot her love of animals and soon decided to become a scientist. She learned how to combine her writing skills with her studies of the environment.

Rachel Carson wrote several books and articles about her observations that helped people become aware of the dangers of pesticides. Pesticides are chemicals used to kill insects on plants. Because of her books, scientists did research and discovered that when used incorrectly, pesticides can be harmful to humans and animals. Since then, laws have been passed that encourage people to be more careful when using pesticides.

This ecologist examines the leaves of a plant to check for damage caused by insects. ▶

Understanding Ecosystems

Use the vocabulary words to complete the sentences.

1. An _____ is a living thing.

2. The scientific study of the relationship between living things and their environment is called _____.

3. A scientist who studies the relationship between living and nonliving things is called an _____.

4. An _____ is everything around an organism.

5. An _____ consists of a group of living and nonliving things that interact with each other in an environment.

What can you do to be a good steward and help the environment?

_____

_____

_____

_____

_____

_____

What do animals eat?

Have you ever skipped a meal? How did you feel later? We get the energy we need to work and play from food. Animals also get the energy they need from food. God designed some animals to eat plants and some animals to eat other animals.

A **producer** is an organism that can make its own food. A tree is a producer. Can you name another producer?

A **consumer** is an organism that eats food. A consumer can eat a producer or another consumer. A bear is a consumer that can eat either a producer, such as a berry, or a consumer, such as a fish. Can you think of another consumer? What does it eat?

An organism that breaks down dead plant and animal material to return it to the soil is called a **decomposer**. A decomposer, such as an earthworm or an ant, helps keep areas clean by getting rid of dead materials.

Animals eat plants and other animals to get the food they need to live. A food chain is the way food passes from one organism to another. A food web is formed when several food chains are connected together. This means that some animals can eat more than just one type of food.

An eagle can eat a snake, a mouse, a chipmunk, or a fish. The food web allows the eagle to find the food it needs. ▶

Understanding a Food Chain

1. Complete the chart by writing a name under each heading.

Decomposer	Producer	Consumer

2. Use the Word Bank to complete the sentence. One word will not be used.

A food chain shows _____ eaten by a

_____ that is eaten by a _____.

Word Bank
berries
fox
frog
rabbit

3. How does a decomposer help an ecosystem?

_____

Why do animals hunt?

Where did your last meal come from? Imagine if you had to go out and hunt for your food. You can be thankful that you do not have to search for your food like many animals do.

God created some animals to hunt for their food. Other animals try to protect themselves from being hunted. A predator is an animal that hunts another animal for food. A fox is a predator of a rabbit because it hunts the rabbit for food. The animal that is hunted is called prey. The rabbit is prey for the fox. Can you name another predator and its prey?

The lion is a predator, and the zebra and giraffe are its prey. ◄

Once an organism has died, there are animals that will eat the remains. An animal that eats dead plants and animals is called a scavenger. Have you ever seen a large number of birds circling high in the air? Many times, these are scavenger birds that have located a dead animal and are waiting until it is safe to fly down and dine! How do these animals help the ecosystem? How are they like decomposers?

Hyenas and vultures are scavengers that eat dead animals.

Identifying Animals

Use the Word Bank to finish each sentence. One word will not be used.

Word Bank	
vulture	prey
mouse	fox
dead	predator

1. A _____ is a predator of a _____.

2. A _____ is a scavenger that eats _____ animals.

3. A fish is _____ for a bear.

4. Why are scavengers important to an ecosystem?

_____

_____

Why do animals compete?

Have you ever had to compete with someone for something? Do you know that plants and animals also compete?

Plants and animals need their own space to live. What happens when too many plants grow in the same area? After a while, some of the plants die because they cannot compete, or work against one another, to get what they need to live. Can you name two animals that might compete against one another for food?

Deer and raccoons live in the forest together, but they do not compete for food.

11

In an ecosystem, many types of organisms must live together. Every organism has a niche which is a special job or role to fill. Animals have niches. Some animals distribute seeds. Other animals help keep areas clean from decaying materials. For example, a squirrel has its own niche in the forest. Acorns provide food for the squirrel. It eats some acorns and buries some. New oak trees grow from some of the acorns that the squirrel buried. Birds, owls, and other squirrels will live in these trees. The squirrel is also food for the owl.

Finding the Right Balance

1. What is the special job or role of an animal called?

_____

2. Name two things animals compete for.

_____ _____

3. How can two animals live in the same habitat without competing for food?

_____

_____

4. Tell what would happen if there were too many animals eating the same food.

_____

_____

How do animals survive?

Adaptation is a way that animals adjust to changes in their environment. In some areas, the weather and temperature change with each season. In winter, animals must find a way to survive the cold temperatures and lack of food. God designed some animals, such as the dormouse, to hibernate or rest through the winter. The dormouse eats extra food and then goes into a period of rest in a nest built underground to keep it warm.

Chipmunks eat a lot all summer so they can hibernate all winter. ▲

Many birds migrate or move from one place to another to avoid these changes. Canada geese fly south to warmer climates. They will fly back to their homes in the spring as the weather changes.

A snowshoe hare sheds its brown, summer fur and grows a thick white coat of fur for winter. This allows the snowshoe hare to blend in with its environment.

The deer, snowshoe hare, and leaf bug are designed in unique ways to blend in with their environments. The way an organism blends in with its environment is called camouflage. Can you describe how camouflage protects these animals?

Deer

Snowshoe hare

Leaf bug

How Animals Survive

Write the letter of the word in the first column next to the correct description in the second column.

A. migrate   _____ The fur of a snowshoe hare changes from brown to white in the winter so the hare can blend in with the snow.

B. camouflage   _____ In the winter, Canada geese fly south where it is warmer and there is more food.

C. hibernate   _____ A dormouse sleeps in a nest underground during the winter.

What happens after a fire?

Have you ever seen an area that has been destroyed by a fire? Have you ever wondered what happens to the animals that once lived there?

During a forest fire, many of the grasses, plants, and trees are destroyed. Droughts, floods, and earthquakes can also destroy habitats. Some animals perish or die during the event. Some animals perish later because of the loss of food. However, many animals are able to relocate or find a new place to live. Squirrels and birds can find new trees to live in. Rabbits and raccoons can find new plants to eat. Bears can find new streams where they can hunt for fish.

It takes many years for the trees, grasses, and plants in a forest to grow back after a fire. Seeds can be scattered by the wind or buried underground. These seeds take root and grow into plants and grass. The nutrients added to soil from the plants help small trees begin to grow. Over time, these small trees grow into larger trees. Animals that lived underground and were protected from the fire can live off stored food until new plants grow.

Observing Animals

1. Name two things that might happen to an animal if its habitat is destroyed.

_____   _____

2. Why would an animal need to relocate after a fire?

_____

_____

3. Number the sentences in order from 1 to 5 telling how a forest grows back after a fire.

_____ The small trees grow into larger trees.

_____ Seeds are scattered by the wind into the devastated area.

_____ Small trees begin to grow.

_____ The plants place nutrients in the soil for small trees to grow.

_____ Seeds take root and grow into plants and grass.

What is the ecosystem all about?

All organisms have four basic needs. They are air, food, water, and shelter. God has designed plants and animals to be dependent on one another to have these needs met.

Look at the pictures of the animals shown on this page. Use a **red** crayon to circle all the predators. Use a **blue** crayon to circle all the prey. Do any of your animals have two circles around them? Why?

Which is which?
Label the pictures. Write a **D** for a decomposer, a **P** for a producer, and a **C** for a consumer.

grass

ant

bear

_____

_____

_____

wolf

berries

owl

_____

_____

_____

Who did what?
Read each sentence. Write the name of the predator and the prey in the blanks.

1. The fish ate the worm.

   predator: _____   prey: _____

2. The mouse was eaten by the cat.

   predator: _____   prey: _____

3. The snake ate the bird that ate the grasshopper.

   predator: _____   prey: _____

   predator: _____   prey: _____

What is happening here?

Match the letter in the first column to the description of what the animal does in each situation.

A-hibernate

B-migrate

C-niche

D-perish

E-compete

F-relocate

_____ The crow moves to a new part of the forest after a fire.

_____ The rabbit and deer want to eat the same grass.

_____ Monarch butterflies fly south in the winter.

_____ An earthworm's job is to be a decomposer.

_____ A dormouse sleeps through the winter.

_____ A fox starves because there is no food left.

Draw **green** arrows to show two food chains.
Draw **orange** arrows to show a food web.

fox

 eagle

mouse

rabbit

clover

berries

Vocabulary Review

Use the Word Bank to complete each sentence.

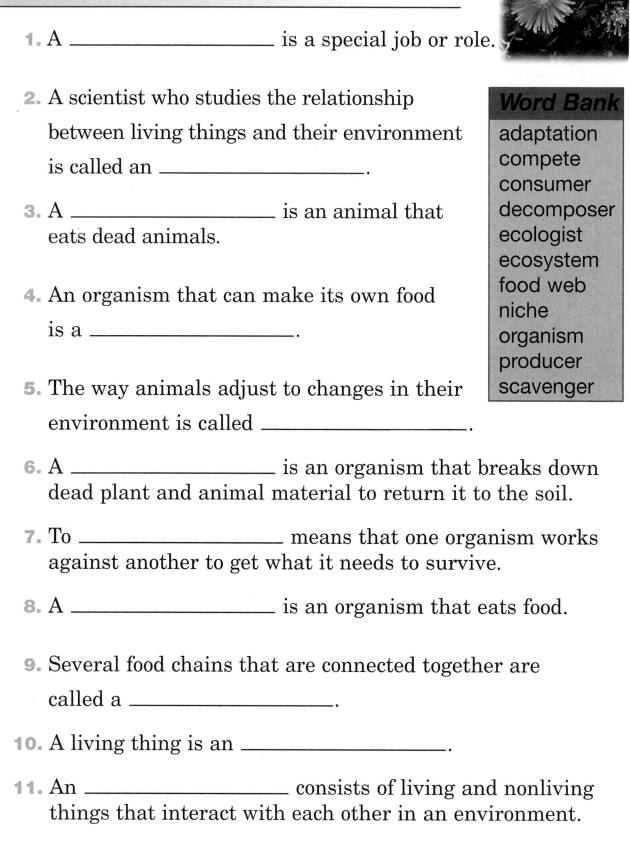

1. A _____ is a special job or role.

2. A scientist who studies the relationship between living things and their environment is called an _____.

3. A _____ is an animal that eats dead animals.

4. An organism that can make its own food is a _____.

5. The way animals adjust to changes in their environment is called _____.

6. A _____ is an organism that breaks down dead plant and animal material to return it to the soil.

7. To _____ means that one organism works against another to get what it needs to survive.

8. A _____ is an organism that eats food.

9. Several food chains that are connected together are called a _____.

10. A living thing is an _____.

11. An _____ consists of living and nonliving things that interact with each other in an environment.

Word Bank

adaptation
compete
consumer
decomposer
ecologist
ecosystem
food web
niche
organism
producer
scavenger

My Booklet about the Life of Plants

Name _____

Chapter 2 Vocabulary Words

- botanist
- botany
- carbon dioxide
- cell membrane
- cell wall
- chlorophyll
- chloroplast
- cytoplasm
- germinate
- heredity
- hybrid
- microscope
- microscopic
- nucleus
- oxygen
- petals
- photosynthesis
- pistil
- plant cutting
- plant division
- plant propagation
- pollen
- pollination
- pollinator
- stamen

How are plants used?

Could the shirt that you are wearing have come from a plant? If it is a cotton shirt, it did! Plants are a very important part of our lives. Can you name one thing that was made from a plant?

Draw a line to match the product to the plant that it comes from.

apple juice   table   T-shirt

Plants need light, warmth, air, water, and nutrients. A plant is made so that it uses all of its parts to help it survive.

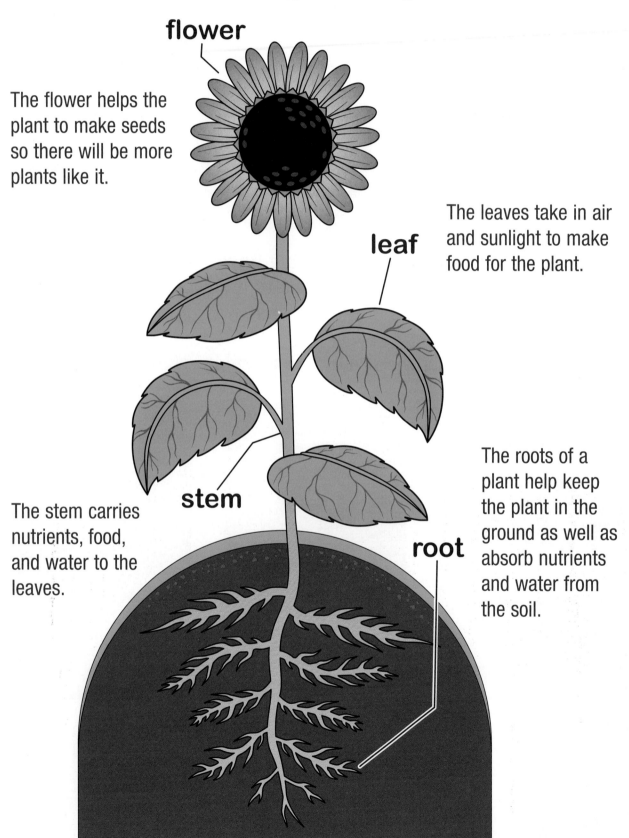

flower

The flower helps the plant to make seeds so there will be more plants like it.

leaf

The leaves take in air and sunlight to make food for the plant.

stem

The stem carries nutrients, food, and water to the leaves.

root

The roots of a plant help keep the plant in the ground as well as absorb nutrients and water from the soil.

A scientist who studies plants is called a botanist. The study of plants is called botany. Botanists study how plants grow and develop. They also collect data that helps them to improve plant growth. They discover new uses for plants and find ways to develop new plants. Other careers in the field of botany are forestry and farming. Can you think of other careers that require knowledge about plants?

Gregor Mendel was a famous botanist who lived in the 1800s. He planted a garden so that he could experiment with plants. Mendel wanted to learn how plants grow and how to produce more plants that look like the parent plants. He used his research to teach other scientists how plants share similar traits with other plants. The experiments and observations that Gregor Mendel did are still studied by scientists today.

TRIVIA

What Bible-time person was a botanist?

See 1 Kings 4:33

Studying Plants

Write the number of the plant function next to its part.

1-helps to make new plants

2-carries water and nutrients to the leaves

3-collects sunlight and air to make food for the plant

4-absorbs water and nutrients for the plant

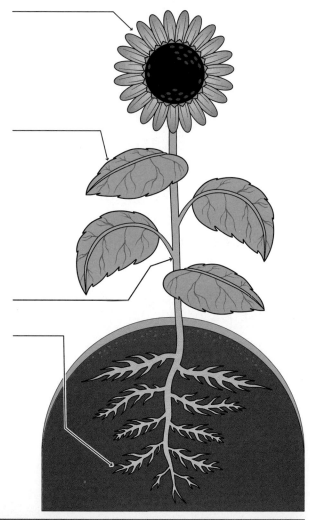

Word Bank				
botanist	leaf	ecology	plant	botany

Use the Word Bank to complete each sentence.
Some words will not be used.

1. A scientist who studies plants is called a _____.

2. Apple juice comes from a _____.

3. The study of plants is called _____.

Do plants breathe?

Take in a big breath. Hold it. Now, blow it out. You have just completed a gas exchange. The air you breathed in was oxygen. Oxygen is a colorless, odorless gas in the air that is needed for most living things to stay alive. The air you blew out was carbon dioxide. Carbon dioxide is a colorless, odorless gas in the air that people and animals breathe out of their lungs.

We breathe oxygen into our lungs and exhale carbon dioxide. Plants, on the other hand, breathe in carbon dioxide and release oxygen into the air. Tiny holes on the surface of a leaf allow the carbon dioxide in the air to enter the plant and allow the oxygen to exit from the plant and enter the air.

People and animals need the oxygen that plants produce. Plants need the carbon dioxide that people and animals produce. God designed this exchange of gases to benefit all living things.

oxygen

carbon dioxide

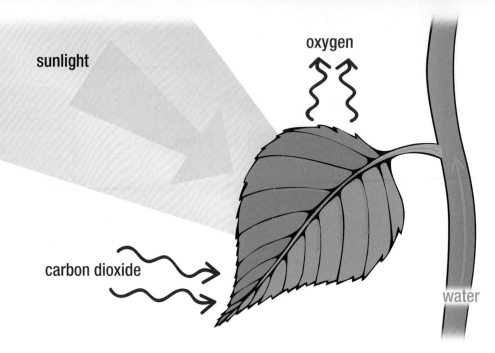

sunlight

oxygen

carbon dioxide

water

Plants use water, carbon dioxide, and sunlight to make food in a process called photosynthesis. When the sun shines on a plant's leaves, chlorophyll, a green coloring in plants, captures the sun's energy. Plants use this energy to make food that helps them live and grow.

Understanding How Plants Make Food

Write the letter of the definition that matches each word.

_____carbon dioxide

_____chlorophyll

_____oxygen

_____photosynthesis

A. The green coloring in a plant that captures the sun's energy.

B. A colorless, odorless gas in the air that is needed for most living things to stay alive.

C. The process that allows green plants to make food from water, carbon dioxide, and sunlight.

D. A colorless, odorless gas in the air that people and animals breathe out of their lungs.

What does a plant cell look like?

A cell is the basic unit of all living things, including the human body. Cells are alive! They eat, breathe, grow, reproduce, and even die. Most cells are microscopic, or too small to be seen without the use of a microscope. A microscope is an instrument that uses lenses and light to make it easier for people to see small objects.

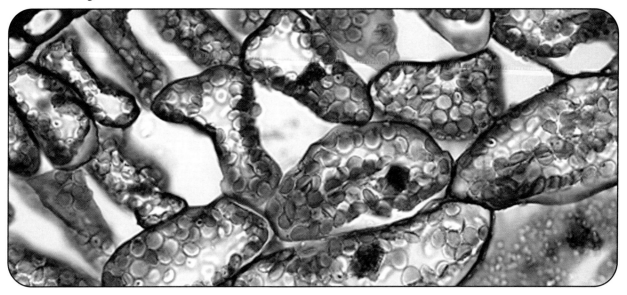

The thin covering of a cell is the cell membrane. It surrounds the entire cell and helps to keep all the parts together. The nucleus is the control center of a cell. It controls all of the cell's activity. Jelly-like material that fills the rest of the inside of a plant cell is called cytoplasm.

Plant cells have a few other parts that make them different from animal cells. A plant cell has a cell wall and chloroplasts. The stiff layer outside the cell membrane of a plant cell is the cell wall. It gives the plant cell its shape. Chloroplasts are tiny green parts inside a plant cell. Chloroplasts contain chlorophyll which gives plants their green color.

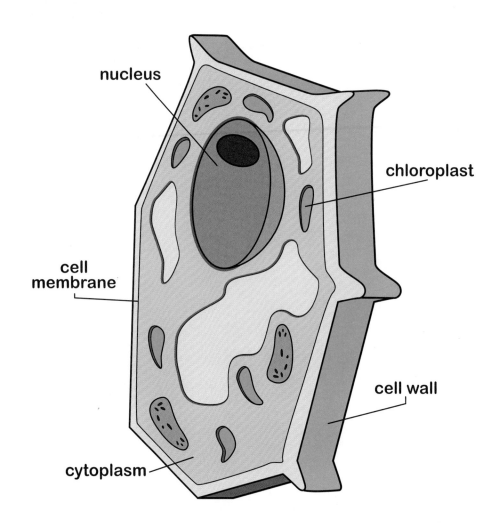

nucleus

chloroplast

cell membrane

cell wall

cytoplasm

Examining Plant Cells

Match the letter of the word to its description.

1. _____ The control center of a cell

2. _____ Tiny green parts inside a plant cell

3. _____ Stiff layer outside the cell membrane of a plant

4. _____ Thin covering of a cell

5. _____ Jelly-like material that fills the inside of a plant cell

A-cell wall

B-cell membrane

C-nucleus

D-cytoplasm

E-chloroplasts

What are the parts of a flower?

Have you ever seen a bumblebee or a butterfly sitting on a beautiful flower? Did you ever wonder what they were doing? Did you know that God designed them to help flowers to make seeds?

stamen

petals

stigma
style ┤ pistil
ovary

ovules

Bumblebees and butterflies are called pollinators. A pollinator is an insect or other animal that carries the pollen to the pistil. The outside parts of a flower that attract pollinators to the flower are called the petals. The colors, the smell, or the shape of the flower attract pollinators. As pollinators drink nectar from the flower, they brush against a stamen, the part of a flower that produces pollen. Pollen is the fine powder in a flower that is needed to make seeds. This pollen sticks to the pollinator's body and is carried to the next flower. When the pollinator reaches the next flower, it brushes against the pistil or the part in a flower where seeds are formed.

The pollen is then joined with the ovule and a new seed is made. In order for flowers to make seeds, they must go through pollination. Pollination is the process by which pollen is carried to the pistil of a flower.

Examining Pollination

Write the numbers 1–7 to show the steps of pollination.

_____ The pollinator brushes against the stamen, and some pollen sticks to its body.

_____ A seed develops.

_____ The pollinator flies to another flower and brushes against the pistil, leaving pollen on it.

_____ A new plant begins to grow.

___1___ A pollinator flies to a flower to taste its nectar.

_____ The seed falls to the ground.

_____ The pollen travels to the ovules.

How do plants make more plants?

God designed plants with the ability to make more plants like themselves. We can make the number of plants increase through plant propagation. Plant propagation means using a part of a plant to increase the number of that plant.

Most plants grow from seeds. When seeds are planted in soil, they will germinate or begin to grow. As the seed grows, it develops into a plant that will eventually grow and look similar to the plant it came from. Flowering plants have a life cycle they go through to develop more flowering plants. A life cycle is all the stages in the life of an organism.

Plant Life Cycle

Plants can also be propagated from plant cuttings. Plant cuttings are parts of a plant such as a leaf, stem, or root that can grow to make another plant.

Dividing a large plant into smaller plants is another form of plant propagation. Plant division is the splitting apart of a plant to produce new plants. Once they are placed in soil, the plant will begin to grow and make more plants of the same kind.

▲From this stem cutting, you can grow a new plant.

Understanding How Plants Grow

Write the numbers from 1–5 showing the life cycle of a flowering plant.

_____ The tiny plant grows into a mature plant. A flower bud develops.

___1___ The seed falls to the ground.

_____ Once the flower is pollinated, the petals die and fall off as the seeds develop inside.

_____ The flower blooms and the pollination process begins.

_____ The seed germinates and tiny roots, leaves, and a stem develop.

Why do some plants look alike?

You see an apple lying on the ground under an apple tree. Do you know where it came from? Of course you do! Apples come from apple trees. You can also tell it came from the apple tree because the rest of the fruit on the tree looks the same as the apple in your hand.

Parent plants will produce plants that look just like them. Heredity is the passing of characteristics from parent to offspring. Characteristics are things like color, size, and shape. A carnation seedling that comes from two red carnations will most likely be red. Why? The characteristic of the color red is passed from the parent to the offspring, or the new plant.

35

Botanists have discovered ways to mix similar plants to get a new plant. This new plant is called a hybrid. A hybrid is a plant that has parents of different varieties, or kinds. Many of our fruits and vegetables are hybrids. For example, a tangelo is a hybrid of a tangerine and a grapefruit. Many types of apples are also hybrids. A Gala apple is a cross of a Cox's Orange Pippin and a Golden Delicious apple. A loganberry is a hybrid of a blackberry and a raspberry.

Understanding Hybrids

Draw a line to match the parent plants with the hybrid fruit it produces.

What have we learned about plants?

Is it possible to look around and not see something that came from a plant? Stop and think about what you eat, what you wear, what you use to do your schoolwork, and even how you travel from place to place. We get food, clothing, furniture, and fuel from plants.

Plants produce oxygen for us to breathe. Plants also depend on us for carbon dioxide, which helps them to make the food they need to grow and develop.

Plants depend on insects and animals to help them form new seeds. Seeds are one way new plants grow. Cuttings from leaves, roots, or even stems will also grow into new plants. In this lesson you'll be reviewing these plant facts—and many others!

What is inside a plant cell?

All living thing are made up of cells. Plant cells have two additional parts that animal cells do not have. The cell wall gives the cell its shape. Plants also have chloroplasts that help the plant make food during photosynthesis.

Match the number of the plant cell part to its description.

1 - nucleus   **4** - cytoplasm
2 - cell membrane **5** - chloroplast
3 - cell wall

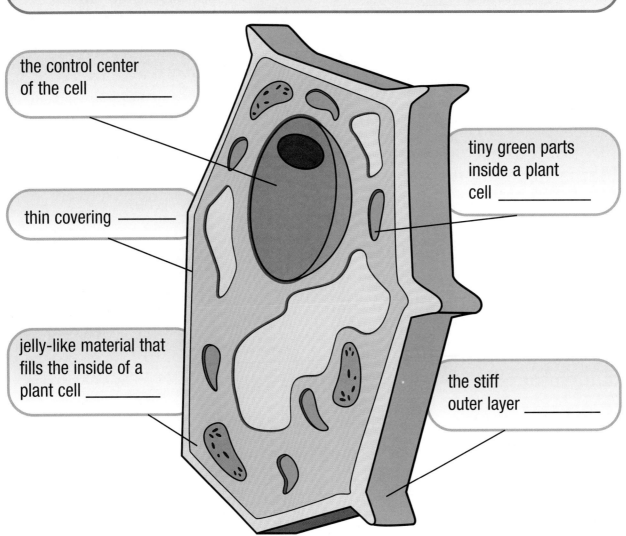

the control center of the cell _____

thin covering _____

jelly-like material that fills the inside of a plant cell _____

tiny green parts inside a plant cell _____

the stiff outer layer _____

What do you remember about plants?

Write **true** or **false** next to each sentence.

1. _____ All plants are only used for clothing.

2. _____ Some plants can have parts cut off to grow new plants.

3. _____ Pollinators do not help carry pollen to other flowers.

4. _____ A botanist studies rocks.

5. _____ A plant gives off carbon dioxide.

Write the numbers from 1–5 to show the life cycle of a flowering plant.

_____ The flower blooms and the pollination process begins.

_____ The tiny plant grows into a mature plant.

_____ The seed germinates and tiny roots, leaves, and a stem develop.

_____ The seed falls to the ground.

_____ Once the flower is pollinated, the petals die and fall off as the seed develops inside.

Vocabulary Review

Use the Word Bank to complete each sentence.

Word Bank

photosynthesis   microscope   botanist
carbon dioxide   oxygen   botany
heredity   microscopic   hybrid   germinate

1. An object that is _____ is too tiny to be seen without the use of a microscope.

2. An odorless, colorless gas in the air that is needed for most living things to stay alive is called _____.

3. The process that allows green plants to make food from water, carbon dioxide, and sunlight is called _____.

4. To begin to grow is to _____.

5. A _____ is a scientist who studies plants.

6. This is an odorless, colorless gas that people and animals breathe out of their lungs. It is _____.

7. The passing of characteristics from a parent to its offspring is called _____.

8. An instrument used to magnify tiny objects is called a _____.

9. The study of plants is called _____.

10. A _____ is a plant that is made from parents of different varieties, or kinds.

My Booklet about Plant Variety

Name _____

bulb	scientific classification
classify	simple plants
phloem	spore
plant biologist	stem
pollination	tuber
pollinator	xylem
root	

Why is there a variety of plants?

When God said, "Let the land produce vegetation," in Genesis 1:11, He created a variety of plants. This is clear in verse 12, where we read about plants and trees "according to their kinds." God did not create just one kind of plant or tree. He created a variety and He "saw that it was good."

Each plant is designed with special characteristics that help it to live in its habitat. Each characteristic has a form and function that helps the plant.

Each plant is designed with unique characteristics that are well-suited for its habitat.

For example, a cactus has a stem that stores water so that it can live in a dry desert. For the shaded tropical rain forest, a philodendron has huge leaves to absorb as much light as possible and a climbing stem that helps the plant to grow toward the light.

One thing that plants need in order to grow is nitrogen. Nitrogen is found in soil. Where nitrogen is scarce, some plants have special ways to get the nitrogen they need. A pitcher plant has a special flower that catches insects and absorbs the nitrogen from their bodies. By God's purposeful design, every plant is perfectly suited to its specific habitat.

A philodendron's large leaves are designed for a rain forest habitat. ▲

A pitcher plant absorbs nitrogen from insects. ▶

What is a plant biologist?

A plant biologist is a scientist who studies how plants live and function in their environment. By observing plants within their specific habitats, we learn what each plant needs. This helps us to do a better job of growing plants for specific needs. For example, the clothes you have on today may be made out of cotton. Plant biologists have developed ways to grow cotton plants so that each plant produces more cotton.

G.A. Eisen / California Academy of Sciences

Alice Eastwood did the work of a plant biologist even though she didn't have a college education. She was born in Toronto, Canada in 1859. She preferred to study plants within their natural habitats, just as plant biologists do today.

She studied plants in the Rocky Mountains, England, Alaska, and the Yukon Territory. She observed plants and collected samples. She recorded details by writing descriptions and drawing pictures in a journal. Other scientists honored her for her work, but that was not Alice Eastwood's motivation. She spent her lifetime studying plants because she loved plants.

Phaeomeria magnifica

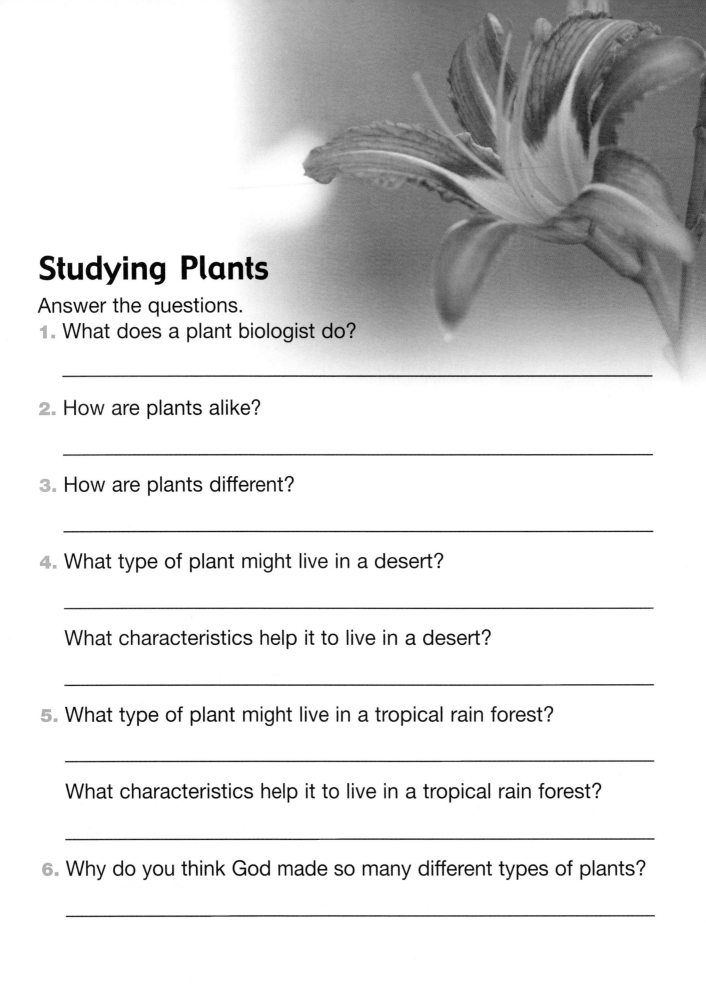

Studying Plants

Answer the questions.

1. What does a plant biologist do?

_____

2. How are plants alike?

_____

3. How are plants different?

_____

4. What type of plant might live in a desert?

_____

What characteristics help it to live in a desert?

_____

5. What type of plant might live in a tropical rain forest?

_____

What characteristics help it to live in a tropical rain forest?

_____

6. Why do you think God made so many different types of plants?

_____

How do roots and stems help plants?

Roots hold the plant in the ground and absorb water and nutrients. However, plants of different kinds have special roots that help them to live in their habitats. A fibrous root is often found in moist areas. It is branched and spreads throughout the soil around the plant. A taproot is found in dry areas. It has a downward-growing, deep, central storage root. Each form helps the plant live in its habitat.

Carrots are taproots.
Basil has fibrous roots.

The stems of plants move water, nutrients, and food to all parts of the plant. All stems contain xylem and phloem tissue. Xylem tissue moves water and nutrients from the roots to all parts of the plant. Phloem tissue moves food, made by photosynthesis in the leaves, to the rest of the plant. However, plants of different kinds have special stems that help them to live in their habitats. In a moist and shaded forest, vine stems wind around or climb on other objects as they reach upward toward the light. In a dry desert, a cactus has a thick stem that stores water.

Some plant stems grow underground. You might be familiar with some already. Onions and potatoes are underground stems. An onion is a bulb and a potato is a tuber. Bulbs and tubers are kinds of underground stems that store water and nutrients and can be divided to make more plants.

How do stems and roots help plants?

How does this stem's special form help this plant in a shaded habitat?

_____

_____

_____

_____

▲ An ivy has a stem that climbs.

How does this root's special form help this plant in a dry habitat?

_____

_____

_____

_____

A yucca has a taproot. ▶

Why are leaves different?

Leaves come in many shapes, textures, and sizes. Leaves can be round or oval, rough or smooth, thick or thin. Every leaf has a form that serves a special function. The leaf's form helps the plant to live in its habitat.

Do you remember the special job the leaf does for the plant? It makes food for the plant through photosynthesis. In order to do its job, the leaf needs water, carbon dioxide, chlorophyll, and light.

In a shady habitat, plants need big, flat leaves that have a lot of exposed surface so they can collect as much light as possible.

In a desert habitat, some plants have thick leaves that store water. A cactus is unique because it makes food in its stem instead of in its leaves. Its sharp spikes protect the cactus from animals that want the food and water stored in the thick stem.

A plant's leaf can help us identify one plant from another. This is helpful because some plants should not be touched or eaten. For example, poison ivy can cause a rash if touched. Some plants, such as castor bean and hemlock, may be deadly if eaten by people. Some houseplants can be harmful if eaten by pets. Farmers need to recognize locoweed since their cattle and horses may die if they eat it. If we can identify harmful plants and avoid them, we can protect ourselves and our animals.

▲Locoweed can hurt horses.

The Purpose of Leaves

Use the Word Bank to complete the sentences. One word will not be used.

Word Bank

habitat
function
form
plant

Every leaf has a _____ that serves a

special _____.

God designed the leaf of each plant to help it live in its

_____.

A philodendron plant has large, flat leaves. Philodendrons often grow in tropical rain forests. How does the form of a philodendron leaf function to help the philodendron to live in its habitat?

_____

_____

_____

Why are flowers different?

Flowers come in many different forms. Each form helps the flower to do its job—to make seed so that new plants will grow. In order to make seed, the flower must be pollinated. God designed a flower to attract moving organisms, called pollinators, to the plant. Pollinators carry the flower's pollen to the pistil, and pollination occurs. The flower provides the pollinator with food such as nectar or pollen. The color, shape, size, and smell of a flower attract specific pollinators. If a flower grows in a forest and has a shape and color that attracts an insect that only lives in a desert, the flower will not be pollinated, no seeds will develop, and the plant will not survive.

The form of a flower attracts a pollinator that lives in the same habitat. Moths prefer white and yellow flowers. Birds and butterflies prefer red and orange. The sweet smell of some flowers attracts birds, bees, and butterflies. Flies are attracted to carrion flowers that smell like rotten meat!

A bee may not fit into a tube-shaped flower, but a butterfly or moth has a long tongue that can reach into the flower. Some other small animals such as bats and hummingbirds are pollinators also.

God designed this wonderful relationship between flowers and pollinators. The pollinators receive food and the flower is pollinated.

Flowers and Pollinators

Use what you have learned to fill in the blanks.

Butterflies and hummingbirds are examples of _____.

A pollinator carries flower pollen to a flower pistil. This process is called _____.

By God's design, both pollinators and plants benefit from their relationship. What does the pollinator receive from the plant? What does the plant receive from the pollinator?

_____

_____

_____

Why are there different colors, shapes, sizes, and fragrances of flowers?

_____

_____

_____

Do all plants have the same parts?

Some plants do not have flowers and do not produce seeds. They are called simple plants. Simple plants are not really simple at all! They are called simple because they have fewer parts. Mosses, liverworts, ferns, and horsetails are simple plants.

Mosses and liverworts are very small plants that do not have roots. Ferns and horsetails are bigger plants, so they need roots and stems for support.

Most simple plants grow in moist places. They make spores instead of seeds. A spore is a microscopic single cell that does not need to be pollinated to become a new plant. Ferns produce spores in clusters on the underside of their leaves. The next time you see a

moss

fern, peek under its leaves. It won't mind! See if you can find the little brown dots. These are its spore clusters. Horsetails have a part that looks like a pine cone that makes spores.

The moist habitat helps the spores to germinate so that eventually there will be new plants. The form of these simple plants helps them live in their habitat.

fern

horsetails

Simple Plants are Unique

Answer these questions about how simple plants are unique.

A fern makes spores on the underside of its _____.

What two plant parts do mosses not have?

_____   _____

Circle the part of the horsetail that makes spores.

Use what you have learned to fill in the blanks.

Some simple plants do not have stems, some do not have roots, and others do not have typical leaves. However, all simple plants do not have _____ and do not make _____.

Why does a plant biologist classify plants?

To classify means to put similar things in the same group. Scientific classification is a system for sorting similar organisms into named groups in order to help scientists communicate quickly and easily. Each group has a Latin name. Latin is a language that was used in the Roman Empire. For this reason, a scientific name can be difficult to understand.

All plants are in a group called Kingdom Plantae. The plants of the kingdom are sorted into smaller groups. The smaller groups are divided again into even smaller groups, and so on. Each group contains plants that are similar in some way. Plant biologists have studied the Latin name of each group. When they hear the name of a plant, they already know a lot about the plant. Scientific classification helps plant biologists to do their job.

Let's look at an example of how a plant biologist might use a plant's name. The Latin word *Acer* is the scientific name for the maple family of trees. Whenever a plant biologist sees the word *Acer* in the name of a plant, he or she knows the plant is a maple tree. One specific tree is named *Acer saccharum*. Seeing its name, the plant biologist knows that this tree is a maple. The plant biologist also knows that the Latin word *saccharum* means *sugar*. The tree's common name is *sugar maple*.

Find the Clues

Can you find clues in the scientific name of each plant that will help you know which plant it is? Draw a line from the plant's scientific name to the plant.

| Daucus carota | Rosa odorata | Zea mays | Iris germanica |

Iris

Corn

Rose

Carrot

How does the scientific classification of plants help plant biologists to do their jobs? _____

_____

_____

_____

Plant Variety Review

Roots and Stems

Use the Word Bank to label the plant part. One word will not be used.

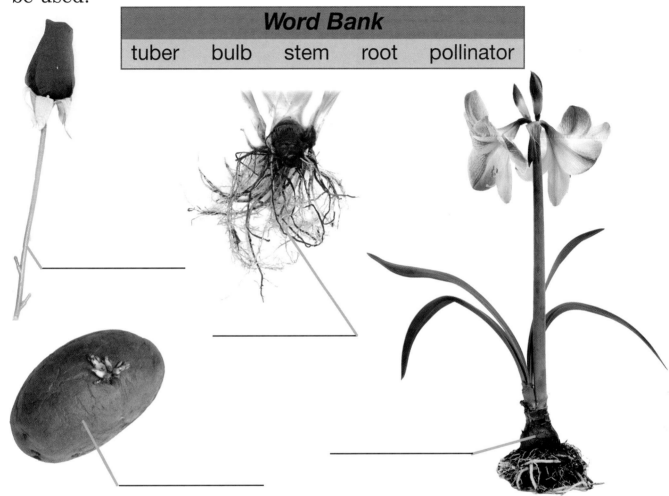

Word Bank				
tuber	bulb	stem	root	pollinator

_____

_____

_____

_____

Roots can be either taproots or fibrous roots. Describe each type of root and the habitat in which we might find it.

taproot _____

_____

fibrous root _____

_____

Leaves

Each plant was designed with a form of leaf that helps the plant live in its habitat. Draw a line from the plant leaf to its habitat.

fern

desert

jade

forest

Explain how the form of each leaf helps the plant live in the habitat that you selected.

fern _____

_____

jade _____

_____

Flowers

Each flower has a form that attracts a pollinator that lives in its habitat. Draw a line from the flower to the pollinator.

hibiscus

fly

skunk cabbage

hummingbird

Explain how the form of each flower helps attract the pollinator to the flower that you selected.

fly _____

_____

hummingbird _____

_____

Simple Plants

Simple plants do not have _____. They do not make seeds. Instead of seeds, simple plants, such as ferns and horsetails, produce _____.

Vocabulary Review

Draw a line from the word to its description.

scientific classification   • to put similar things in the same group

• the process by which pollen is carried to the pistil of a flower

pollinator

• the insect or animal that carries the pollen to the pistil

pollination

• a system for sorting similar organisms into named groups in order to help biologists communicate quickly and easily

spore

• a microscopic single cell that does not need to be pollinated to become a new plant

classify

• holds the plant in the ground and absorbs water and nutrients

plant biologist

• a scientist who studies plants in their own habitat

stem

• supports the plant and moves water, nutrients, and food to the rest of the plant

xylem

• moves water and nutrients from the roots to the rest of the plant

phloem

• moves food, made by photosynthesis in the leaves, to the rest of the plant

root

My Booklet about Matter

Name _____

Chapter 4 Vocabulary Words

atom	metric system
chemical reaction	mixture
chemist	molecule
conservation of matter	properties
cycle of matter	pure substance
deposition	solid
gas	solution
liquid	state of matter
mass	sublimation
matter	substance
measurement system	

How are objects different?

All of the physical objects around us are made of matter. Matter is defined as anything that occupies space and that we can see, smell, taste, hear, or touch. We use our five senses to gather information about the characteristics of the matter around us. For example, a flower is a form of matter that is colorful and has a sweet scent. Some forms of matter we can eat, like grapefruit. Other matter, like air, cannot be seen, but we can hear air move when the wind blows. Some matter feels hard, while other matter feels soft.

The basic component of matter is the atom. When two or more atoms are connected together, they form a molecule. The amount of matter in an object is called mass.

The unique characteristics of matter are called properties. Learning to identify the properties of matter helps us to tell objects apart and understand what matter is made of.

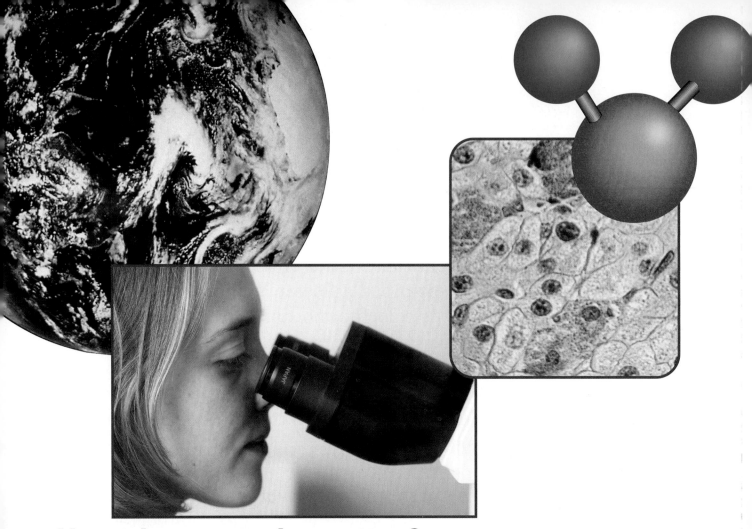

How do we study matter?

"So that people may see and know, may consider and understand, that the hand of the Lord has done this, that the Holy One of Israel has created it." (Isaiah 41:20)

In this verse, we see that God has equipped us to study the world around us so that we may know more about Him and His Creation.

See: Observe with our eyes.
Know: Use all of our senses together.
Consider: Think about what we observe.
Understand: Gain insight about the natural world.

Today, scientists use a very similar process when they study nature. As we observe, study, and think about matter, we will understand more and more about God's creative power.

Who studies matter?

A scientist who studies the properties of matter is called a chemist. Chemists study what objects are made of, how materials change, and how matter interacts with other kinds of matter.

Chemists help keep the environment clean by measuring chemical run-off of fertilizers on farms. They also design better kinds of batteries for cellular phones and computers. Chemists even help the police solve crimes by analyzing the samples that detectives collect at crime scenes.

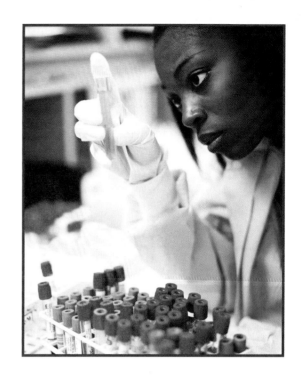

◀ By studying God's creation, chemists have learned about matter and have created new materials such as dyes, plastics, and medicines.

Properties of Objects

Properties are the unique characteristics of matter. Identify the properties of each of the following objects. There may be more than one correct answer.

- ○ Fast
- ○ Slow

- ○ Dry
- ○ Moist

- ○ Brittle
- ○ Unbreakable
- ○ Dark
- ○ Transparent

- ○ Square
- ○ Triangle
- ○ Circle
- ○ Line

- ○ Black
- ○ White
- ○ Gray

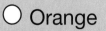
- ○ Orange
- ○ Red
- ○ Yellow
- ○ Green
- ○ Sour
- ○ Bitter
- ○ Salty
- ○ Sweet

How big is "big"?

When a group of people agree to measure things using a collection of specific standards, it is called a measurement system. The measurement system in the United States uses the foot as a standard for length. The measurement system that uses the meter as the standard of length is called the metric system. It is used throughout much of the world and by many scientists.

The metric system allows scientists to describe the properties of matter accurately using words and numbers. They have been able to measure the length of a living cell, the volume of a swimming pool, the mass of a rock, and the temperature of the sun because they agree upon standards for each of the measurements.

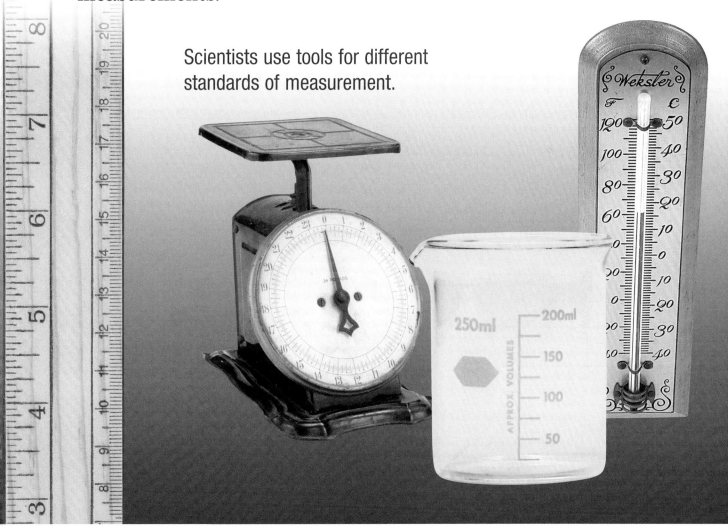

Scientists use tools for different standards of measurement.

Standards of Measurement

Here are some of the common standards of measurement used in the metric system:

> **Length:** meter   **Volume:** liter
> **Temperature:** degree Celsius   **Mass:** gram

For each of the following pictures, write the standards of measure you would use to describe the properties of matter more accurately.

Did you know?
In Biblical times, the standard length of measurement was the cubit, which is about half a meter.

Where does everything around us come from?

The Bible tells us that God created all the matter in the universe. He also created certain laws that define how matter is to behave. One law that God established is called the conservation of matter, which means that matter can change form, but it cannot be created or destroyed. All the matter around us will eventually rearrange into different kinds of matter.

▼ Trees are cut down to make paper and furniture.

◀ The wood is pressed into rolls of paper.

◀ By recycling paper, we can cut down fewer trees.

One way matter is conserved in nature is through cycles. A cycle of matter is a process in which matter undergoes change and eventually goes back to its original form. The water cycle is the process of water evaporating from the earth's surface, forming clouds, and returning to the earth through precipitation. Another cycle occurs when plants take in carbon dioxide and release oxygen while animals and humans breathe in oxygen and release carbon dioxide.

▲ The exchange of oxygen and carbon dioxide between plants and us is an example of a cycle of matter.

How do cycles of matter show the wisdom of God?

_____

_____

_____

_____

_____

_____

What are the states of matter?

A state of matter is the physical property that defines how molecules are arranged in the matter.

A solid is matter whose molecules are packed close together and can barely move. Solids maintain a definite shape and a definite volume.

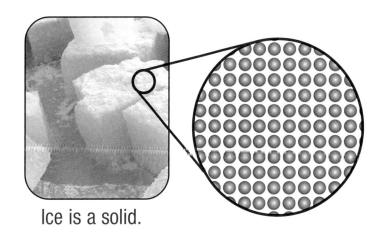
Ice is a solid.

A liquid is matter whose molecules are packed close together, but the molecules move fast enough to have some freedom and not be confined to certain positions. Liquids have a definite volume, but their shape changes to fit the container they are in.

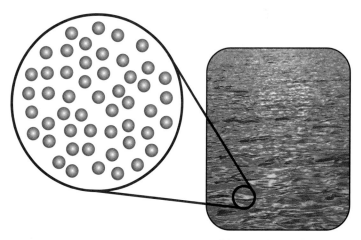
Water is a liquid.

A gas is matter whose molecules move so fast that they fly away from one another in random directions. Gases have no definite shape or volume.

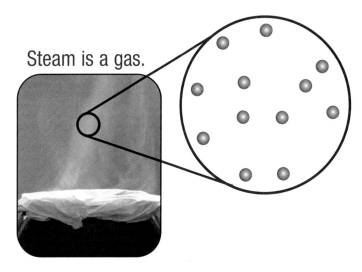
Steam is a gas.

What about changes in the states of matter?

There are six processes that describe changes in states of matter. You probably already know the first four.

Melting: when a solid becomes a liquid

Freezing: when a liquid becomes a solid

Evaporation: when a liquid becomes a gas

Condensation: when a gas becomes a liquid

Sublimation: when a solid becomes a gas

Deposition: when a gas becomes a solid

How does water change?

Complete the diagram below by writing the name of the change that water is undergoing in the arrows. A red arrow means it is being heated while a blue arrow means it is being cooled.

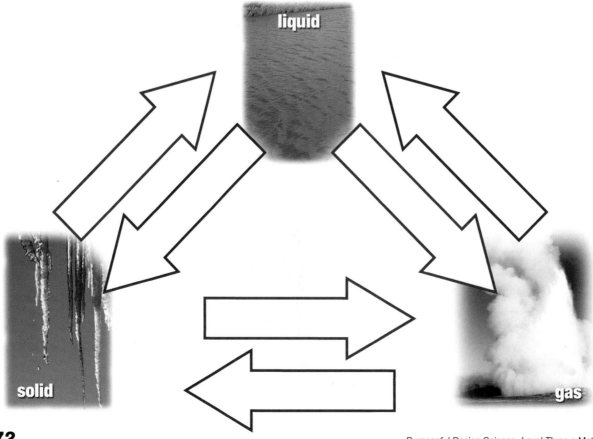

How does matter mix together?

A substance is matter with a unique arrangement of atoms that makes it different from other kinds of matter. When matter contains only one kind of substance, it is a pure substance. Many of the forms of matter that exist in our world do not exist by themselves. Instead, they exist as a mixture of two or more substances. A mixture is any combination of substances that can be physically separated. For instance, distilled water is pure because all of the minerals have been separated from the water. Tap water is a mixture because it contains water and minerals.

▲ You may not see them, but tap water contains minerals.

Most of the foods you eat are mixtures of substances. Salad, hamburgers, soups, and pies are mixtures. Most drinks are mixtures. Milk, juices, and soft drinks are mixtures too. When you smell food and drinks, your nose is usually responding to a mixture of smells and not just one smell.

A solution is a special kind of mixture. A solution is a mixture that acts like a pure substance.

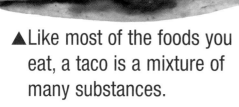

▲ Like most of the foods you eat, a taco is a mixture of many substances.

What's in the food?

For each of the pictures below, write the substances that are present. Indicate whether it is a pure substance, a mixture, or a solution.

Hamburger ingredients:

_____

_____

○ Pure   ○ Mixture   ○ Solution

Salt ingredients:

_____

_____

○ Pure   ○ Mixture   ○ Solution

Tea ingredients:

_____

_____

○ Pure   ○ Mixture   ○ Solution

How does matter change?

The law of the conservation of matter says that matter can change form, but cannot be created or destroyed. When matter changes its physical state from a solid, liquid, or gas to another state, the molecules stay intact.

▲ A chemical reaction turns batter into muffins.

But what happens when the molecules change? When the atoms within a molecule are rearranged to make new molecules with different properties, a chemical reaction has occurred.

There are lots of chemical reactions in our world. Have you ever seen a campfire? When the wood is burned, the molecules in the wood react with oxygen in the air to make carbon dioxide and water. When food is cooked, the molecules within the food get rearranged into different molecules that change the form of the food. When food is eaten, the molecules in the food are changed to smaller molecules, releasing energy.

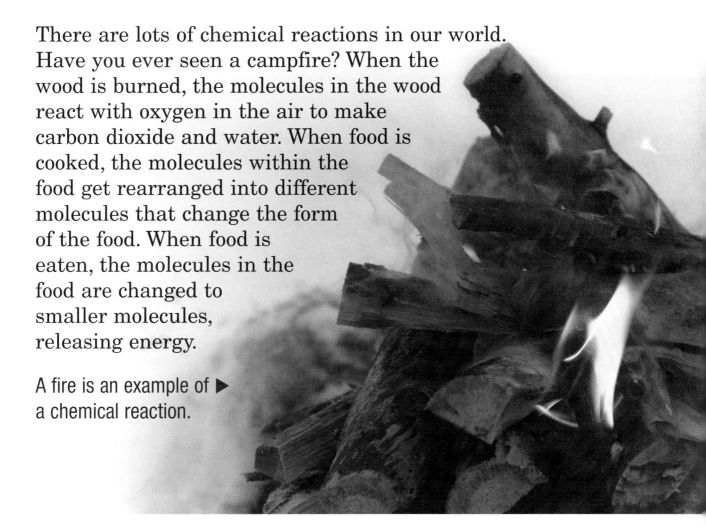

A fire is an example of ▶ a chemical reaction.

Before and After

Here are some examples of chemical reactions taking place. Draw an arrow from the item in the circle to the item it changed into in the box.

All About Matter

In this chapter, you have learned about some of the properties of the matter that exists all around us. Let's review what you have learned.

Matter has many different properties. From the list of properties below, draw a line from the picture to the property that best describes the object.

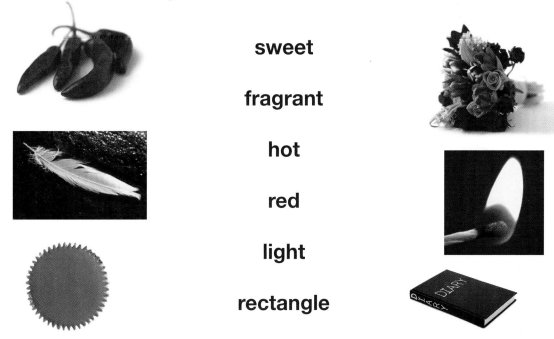

sweet

fragrant

hot

red

light

rectangle

Use the Word Bank to complete the sentences.

1. A ruler is used to measure _____.

2. A measuring cup is used to measure _____.

3. A thermometer is used to measure _____.

4. A scale is used to measure _____.

Word Bank			
temperature	length	mass	volume

In the following diagrams, write **gas**, **liquid**, or **solid** in the blanks.

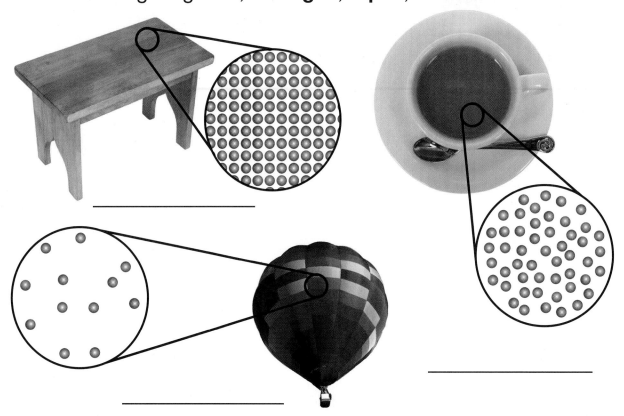

_____

_____

_____

In the following diagram, identify each change in the state of matter using the Word Bank below. Write your answers inside the arrows.

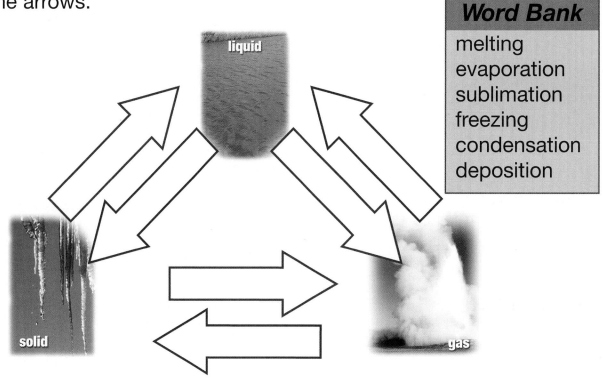

liquid

solid

gas

Next to each picture, write an **M** if it is a mixture and a **P** if it is a pure substance.

_____

_____

_____

_____

_____

_____

Match the words below with the following definitions about changes in matter:

chemical reaction

> the rearrangement of atoms within molecules to form new molecules with different properties

conservation of matter

> the physical property that defines how molecules are arranged within matter

state of matter

> matter can change form, but cannot be created or destroyed

Vocabulary Review

Use the Word Bank to complete the sentences.

1. A _____ is a collection of
   specific standards that a group of people agree to use for
   measuring things.

2. Matter with a unique arrangement of atoms that
   makes it different from other kinds of matter is
   called a _____.

3. Anything that occupies space that we can see, smell, taste,
   hear, or touch is called _____.

4. A scientist who studies the properties of matter is called a
   _____.

5. The unique characteristics of matter are called _____.

6. A combination of two or more substances that can be
   physically separated is a _____.

7. A _____ is a mixture that acts like a pure
   substance.

8. A process of matter undergoing a change and eventually going
   back to its original form is called a _____ of matter.

Word Bank			
measurement system	substance	matter	mixture
chemist	properties	cycle	solution

My Booklet about Motion and Force

Name _____

angular motion	periodic motion
compound machine	physicist
force	power
friction	rotational motion
gravity	simple machine
linear motion	velocity
motion	work

What is motion?

The change in an object's location over a certain amount of time is called motion.

How would you describe the motion of a jet traveling at 600 miles per hour? You could point to the sky and say, "It took three seconds to get from there to there!" That says how far you saw the jet travel and how long it took. But you wouldn't be able to say exactly how fast it was traveling unless you knew the actual distance the jet traveled and the actual time it took to fly that distance.

Linear motion is the motion of an object along a straight line. A car driving down the road or a rocket shot into space are examples of linear motion. There are two types of linear motion. The first is horizontal motion, which is motion that is forward, backward, left, or right. The second is vertical motion, which is up-and-down motion.

▲ The horizontal motion of a car is along a straight line.

The vertical motion of a rocket is also along a straight line. ▶

How do we measure linear motion?

To measure the linear motion of a car, for instance, we need to measure how far it moves in how much time. The velocity is the distance that an object travels over a certain amount of time. Velocity is also called speed. If you are in a car traveling at 60 miles per hour (mph), it will take you one hour to travel 60 miles.

Famous Physicists

A scientist who studies motion is called a physicist. Some famous physicists are Leonardo da Vinci, Galileo Galilei, Sir Isaac Newton, and Albert Einstein.

Math and Motion

Answer the following questions. You will need to calculate your answers.

1. Bill decides to go for a 3-hour bike ride. How far will he travel if the average speed of his bike is 11 miles per hour?

   _____ x _____ = _____

2. Jenny is a marathon runner. Her average running speed is 9 miles per hour. If she runs for 2 hours, how far can she go?

   _____ x _____ = _____

What is angular motion?

Angular motion is the motion of an object around a central point. If you draw a line from the object to the center, move the object, and then draw another line, the two lines form an angle.

When you ride on a carousel, you move around in a circle and always at the same distance from the center. This motion is called rotational motion. Rotational motion is the motion of an object in a complete circle. When an object returns to the place where it started, it has completed one rotation.

Top view

Another type of angular motion is periodic motion. **Periodic motion** is the back-and-forth motion of an object from a central point. The amount of time it takes for an object to return to where it started is called a period.

The amusement park ride acts as a pendulum. ▶

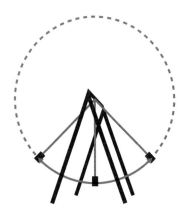

Photo courtesy of Six Flags Elitch Gardens

Rotational or periodic?

Identify the type of angular motion you see in each photo. Write **rotational** or **periodic** in the blank next to each photo.

_____   _____

_____

What kinds of forces are there?

A force is the push or pull of one object on another object. The force that resists the motion of one object against another is called friction.

When we push or pull an object across the floor, we are applying a force to it. For the object to move, the force we apply must be stronger than the friction from the floor that pushes back. If the force we apply to the object is stronger than the friction of the floor, the object moves.

▲The sled moves because the pulling force is stronger than the force of friction.

Forces can also exist between two objects that are not in contact. These forces push or pull objects from a distance.

Gravity is the force pulling together all objects in the universe. Gravity pulls us toward the floor, but the floor pushes back with an equal force. We don't float into space or sink into the floor because these forces are equal. When we throw a ball, the horizontal motion stays the same but the vertical motion changes because gravity pulls the ball to the ground.

▲The push of an applied force makes the plane go forward, but gravity will pull the plane to the ground.

Identifying Forces

For the pictures below, draw arrows of the opposing forces involved in each.

What is work?

When we lift a pencil, ride a bike, run in a race, or eat dinner, the muscles in our bodies move our arms or legs over a certain distance. Work is being done and energy is being transferred. Work is using a force on an object to make it move.

Power is the amount of work done over a certain amount of time. A car has more power than a bicycle because it accomplishes the same amount of work in less time.

How much effort?

Sometimes, we can spend a lot of energy on a task and have very little to show for it. Have you ever noticed that riding your bike uphill takes more effort than riding downhill? It takes more effort to ride uphill because you must overcome the force of gravity.

For each pair of photos, circle the task that takes more effort.

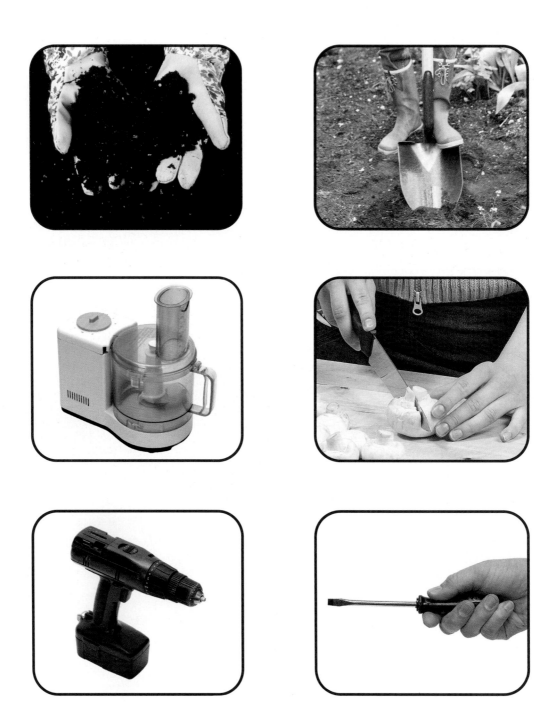

Sir Isaac Newton

Who was Isaac Newton?

Sir Isaac Newton (1642–1727) was one of the greatest physicists who ever lived. He studied many different areas in science. He is famous for his study of motion and his discovery of laws that describe how objects move. Newton also had a deep faith in God, believed in the story of Creation, and studied the Bible daily. Newton believed science and mathematics supported the Bible because he never found any conflicts between his science and his faith.

Newton's First Law

This lesson focuses on Newton's first law of motion:

Every object at rest stays at rest and every object in motion remains in motion unless they are acted upon by outside forces.

For instance, a rocket on the launch pad will not move until an outside force acts on it, which is the thrust from the burning rocket fuel.

Photo courtesy of NASA

Newton's First Law in Action

The ball is at rest. What outside force could make it move?

_____

_____

The pins and ball are in motion. What force could make them slow down?

_____

_____

The boulder is at rest. What outside force could make it move?

_____

_____

The go-cart is in motion. What force could make it slow down?

_____

_____

What is a simple machine?

A simple machine is a tool that requires only one force to be used. The six types of simple machines are the lever, wheel and axle, pulley, inclined plane, wedge, and screw.

A lever is a rigid bar that rotates about a fixed point.

A wheel and axle turns the rotation of the wheel into a force on an axle.

A pulley is a wheel with a rope that passes over it to lift objects.

A screw is an inclined plane wrapped around a wheel and axle.

A wedge is made from back-to-back inclined planes.

An inclined plane is a slanted surface.

Identifying Simple Machines

Draw a line from the simple machine to the correct tool.

lever

wheel and axle

pulley

inclined plane

wedge

screw

A combination of two or more simple machines is called a compound machine.

What simple machines can you find in this photo?

_____

_____

_____

_____

_____

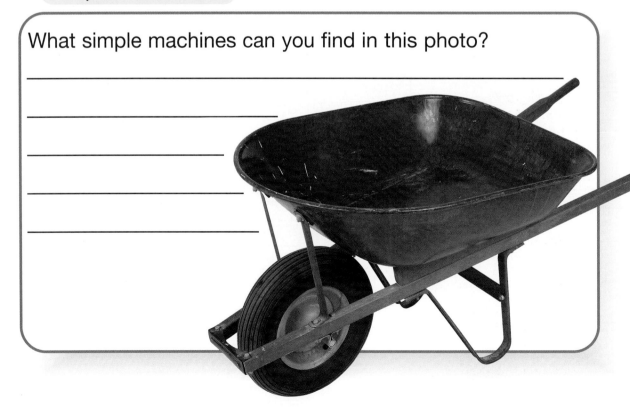

How do things move?

In this chapter, you have studied several different kinds of motion, forces, and machines.

There are a few different ways that objects can move. Linear motion is the motion of an object along a straight line. Angular motion is the motion of an object around a central point.

Examine each of the following pictures. In the blank next to each photo, write an **L** if the object experiences linear motion and an **A** if it experiences angular motion. More than one answer may be correct.

Draw a line from the word to its definition.

linear motion — the back-and-forth motion of an object from a central point

rotational motion — the motion of an object along a straight line

periodic motion — the motion of an object in a complete circle

Examine each of the following pictures. In the blank next to each photo, write an **R** if the object experiences rotational motion and a **P** if it experiences periodic motion.

_____

_____

_____

The force that resists the motion of one object against another is called friction. The force pulling together all objects in the universe is gravity. In the following photos, draw an arrow to show the force of friction and gravity.

98

Purposeful Design Science, Level Three • Motion and Force

Work is using a force on an object to make it move. Circle the process that takes less effort.

Power is the amount of work done over a certain amount of time. Circle the object that has more power.

truck

wheelbarrow

A simple machine is a tool that requires only one force to be used. A combination of two or more simple machines is called a compound machine. Next to each picture, write an **S** if it is a simple machine and a **C** if it is a compound machine.

Vocabulary Review

Use the Word Bank to complete the sentences.

Word Bank
force
friction
gravity
motion
power
velocity
work

1. Using force on an object to make it move is

   _____.

2. The _____ of an object is the
   change in its location over a certain amount of
   time.

3. In the universe, _____ is the force pulling
   together all objects.

4. The push or pull of one object on another object is

   _____.

5. The _____ of an object is the distance that
   an object travels over a certain amount of time.

6. The amount of work done over a certain amount of time is

   _____.

7. The force of _____ is the force that resists
   motion of one object against another.

My Booklet about Electricity

Name _____

attract	insulator
circuit	parallel circuit
conductor	repel
electric current	resistor
electric discharge	series circuit
electrical engineer	static electricity
electricity	switch

What is electricity?

Electricity makes things work. Appliances just sit there and do nothing, but as soon as you plug them into an electrical outlet and turn them on, they have power and can do things like play music, wash clothes, and dry hair. Because electricity is such a big part of your life, you might not even realize how much you depend on it.

For example, the lamp you turned on this morning when you got out of bed was probably plugged into an outlet. So are computers, refrigerators, and microwaves. In fact, it is very likely that there is a least one electrical appliance in every room of your house! You know that appliances with plugs need electricity. But did you know that things that run on batteries use electricity also? Batteries generate electricity, so that means that flashlights, cell phones, and hand-held video games all use electricity too!

Modern cities depend on electricity.

God has given people the ability to learn about the universe He created. Even though scientists know some things about electricity, their knowledge is very tiny compared to what God knows. As you study electricity, you will learn a little bit more about an important aspect of this world that God has created for you to live in!

All physical things are made of matter. Matter is made of tiny particles called atoms. These atoms are made of even tinier particles that have electric charges. Electric charges can be either positive (+) or negative (–). The form of energy that comes from these charged particles is called electrical energy.

Matter is made of tiny particles called atoms.

Most objects are neutral. This means that they have an equal number of positive and negative charges. However, these charges don't always stay in one place. The negative charges can sometimes move or flow from one object to another. The flow of charged particles is called electricity.

These objects are neutral. They have an equal number of positive and negative charges.

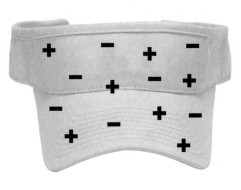

Rubbing a balloon with wool ▶ causes negative charges to build up on the balloon. This results in more positive charges on the wool. Both objects are "charged" with static electricity.

Sometimes electrical charges build up on the surface of an object. The sudden flow of charged particles from this buildup is called static electricity. You've probably seen static electricity in action if you have ever rubbed a balloon against your head.

Negative charges move from your hair to the balloon. Now there are more positive charges in your hair and more negative charges on the balloon.

You probably noticed that this causes pieces of your hair to stand straight up and "stick" to the balloon. This happens because objects with opposite charges pull towards each other or attract. Objects with the same charges push away from each other or repel.

So now that you know a little about how static electricity works, let's see if you can use it!

Why do socks stick to clothes when they come out of the dryer?

Remember, clothes are made of matter. If they rub together, negative charges from a sock can move to another piece of clothing.

Why is this sock sticking to these pants? _____

_____

_____

_____

What kind of electricity is built up on the surfaces of these clothes?

_____

Because modern civilization depends so heavily upon electricity, scientists are constantly developing new ways to use it. Electrical engineers are people who design new technology that uses electrical energy. Some things they have designed already are electric motors, cars, aircraft, computers, robots, and global positioning systems. What kinds of new things do you think they will develop in the future?

Why do we sometimes get an electric shock?

Have you ever touched a doorknob and felt a shock? Or maybe you have touched another person's hand and felt a zap? This usually happens after you have walked across a carpet. Knowing what you know about static electricity, can you think of an explanation for why this happens?

When your shoes rub against the carpet, negative charges move from the rug to your shoes. They then move from your shoes to your body. This charges your body with static electricity. Electrical charges don't stay in one place for very long. Sooner or later, the charges have to move. Some of the charges may flow into the air. Other charges will flow from your body through the air to another object. This movement of charges is called an electric discharge.

So why do you sometimes feel an electric shock when you touch metal, but not when you touch wood? Static electricity only flows through certain materials. Metal is a conductor. It allows electricity to flow through it easily. Wood is an insulator. It does not allow electricity to flow through it easily. Can you think of any other materials that are conductors or insulators?

▲Water is a conductor.

Will you get a shock?

Objects made of conductors such as metal allow electricity to flow through them easily. Objects made of insulators like wood or plastic do not allow electricity to flow through them easily. Circle the objects that could give you an electric shock.

How does electricity make things work?

You know that items such as your computer, your television, and your flashlight all run on electricity. But how exactly does electricity make them work?

Electrical devices use an electric current for power. An electric current is the flow of electricity through a conductor. In this form, negative electric charges flow continuously along a path called a circuit. The charges flow through the circuit in a similar way to how water flows through a garden hose.

Circuits can be either closed or open. Electricity can only flow through a closed circuit. This means there are no breaks in the circuit. If you connect a battery to a light bulb with two wires in a closed circuit, the bulb will light up. If you disconnect a wire, and the circuit is open, then electricity cannot flow through the circuit. The bulb will not light up.

closed circuit

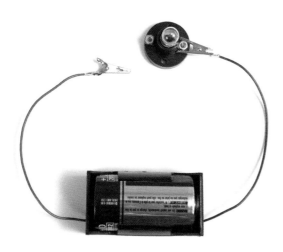

open circuit

109

A switch is a device that can open or close a circuit. Turning the switch on closes the circuit and causes the bulb to light. Turning the switch off opens the circuit and the bulb will not light. Can you think of a reason why switches are useful?

switch on

switch off

How does a flashlight work?

When you turn a flashlight on, the switch moves and you close the circuit. This causes the bulb to light. When you turn the flashlight off, the switch makes a gap and the circuit is open. Since electricity can no longer flow through the circuit, the bulb does not light.

Draw a circle around the place where the switch opens the circuit. Draw a square around the place where the switch closes the circuit.

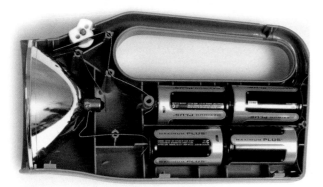

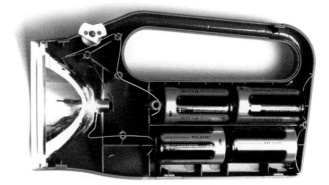

What are different kinds of circuits?

An electric current needs a path to follow. The path that it follows is called a circuit. A closed circuit allows electricity to flow through it. An open circuit does not.

Circuits are kind of like mazes. Sometimes there is only one path electricity can follow. This is called a series circuit. If there is a break in any part of this circuit, the electricity stops flowing. For example, if you removed light bulb B, light bulb A would go out.

Series circuit

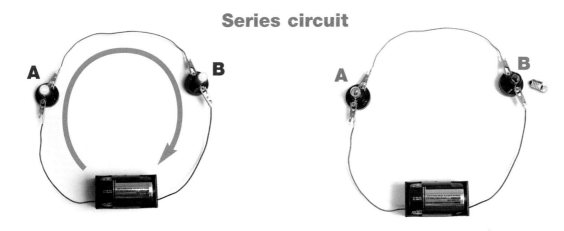

Another kind of circuit is a parallel circuit. In this type of circuit, electricity has more than one path that it can follow. For example, if you removed light bulb A, light bulb B would stay lit, because there is another closed circuit for the electricity to flow through.

Parallel circuit

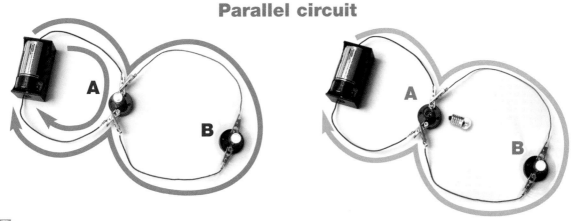

Circuits

Electrical outlets in homes are connected by parallel circuits.
Can you imagine what would happen if they weren't?

Describe what would happen if the electrical outlets in your home
were connected in a series circuit and one light bulb burned out.

_____

_____

What would happen when you turned on one light switch?

_____

_____

Look at these Christmas lights and identify the ones connected
by a series circuit and the ones connected by a parallel circuit.
Explain your answers.

_____

_____

_____

_____

_____

How do we use electricity?

We use electricity for a lot of things, but probably one of the main things we depend on it for is to produce light. You can probably walk into any room of your house, flip a switch, and immediately have light.

So how exactly does electricity make a light bulb light up? You know that electricity flows through a circuit. As it flows through an incandescent light bulb, the current passes through a filament. This causes the filament to get very hot, start to glow, and give off light.

Why does the filament get so hot? It is made of a material that resists, but does not stop, the electric current. This resistance produces heat and eventually light. In incandescent bulbs, filaments are made of tungsten, a metal that resists electric current. Materials that resist electric current are called resistors.

INCANDESCENT BULB

filament

113

Another type of light bulb is a fluorescent bulb. Fluorescent bulbs contain neon or argon gas with small amounts of mercury gas. As electricity enters the bulb, it encounters these particles of gas, causing the gas to give off ultraviolet light. When this light strikes the coating of the bulb, white light is produced.

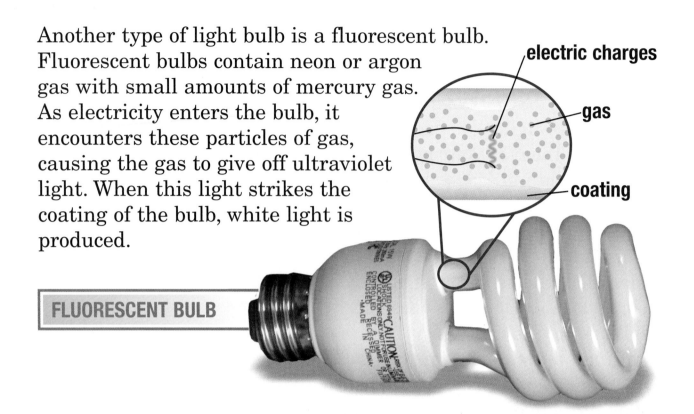

electric charges

gas

coating

FLUORESCENT BULB

Incandescent or fluorescent?

Incandescent bulbs change electrical energy into heat and light. The problem is they produce much more heat than they do light. That is why incandescent bulbs get so hot. All the heat these bulbs produce is wasted energy.

On the other hand, fluorescent bulbs use electricity to change one form of light into another form of light. They produce much less heat and cost much less to operate than incandescent bulbs.

Compare incandescent and fluorescent bulbs. Which bulb is more efficient?

_____

_____

_____

How can we be safe around electricity?

Playing with static electricity and tiny batteries is fun and safe, but other kinds of electricity are very dangerous. The shock a person could receive from an electrical outlet or a power line could seriously injure or kill him or her. It is always important to be very careful around electricity.

Electricity is always trying to discharge into the ground because the earth can absorb the charge. It will always take a shortcut if it is available. Water is a good conductor of electricity. Since our bodies are made mostly of water, we can be conductors too! If you touch an electrical circuit, electricity will use you as a shortcut to get to the ground.

You are not the only thing electricity can flow through! Anything that is made of metal or can get wet can be a conductor. A tree branch, a ladder, or a kite string can conduct electricity. Keep the safety tips on the next page in mind to stay safe around electricity.

▲ Never fly a kite near power lines.

Safety Tips

1. Only put plugs in electrical outlets. Inserting other objects into the outlet holes can cause serious injury or death.

2. Keep all electrical devices away from water. Electricity can jump from the device to the water and shock you.

3. Never use appliances that have frayed wires. If you touch an exposed wire, you could be shocked.

4. Don't overload outlets with too many plugs. This can cause a short circuit or an electrical fire.

5. Stay away from downed power lines and objects that are close to the power line. The electricity in these lines is very strong and can seriously hurt or kill you.

Be Safe

Circle safe uses of electricity. Draw an X over unsafe uses of electricity.

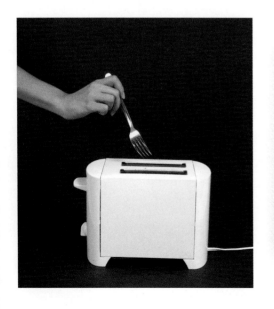  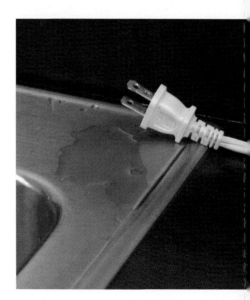

Static Electricity

These balloons are charged with static electricity. Draw arrows to show if the charges cause them to attract or repel each other.

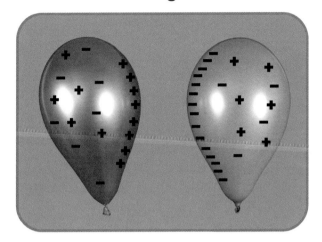

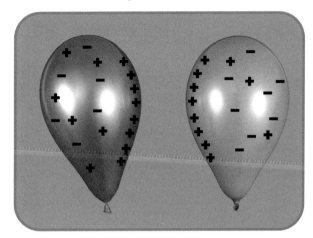

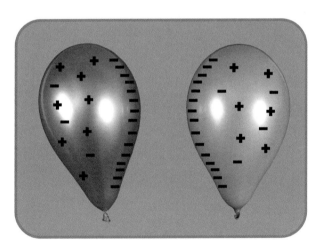

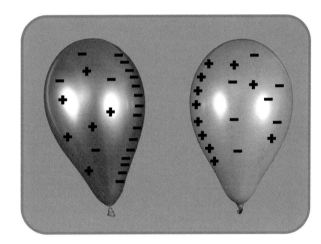

Explain how static electricity is causing this balloon to stick to the wall.

_____

_____

_____

_____

_____

_____

Conductor or Insulator?

Write a **C** in the box by objects that are conductors. Write an **I** in the box by objects that are insulators.

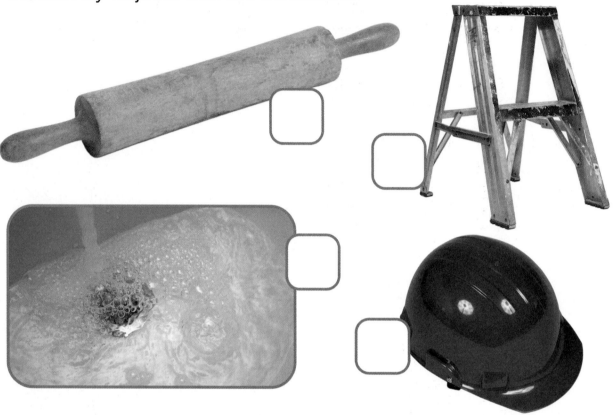

Write **T** if the statement is true or **F** if the statement is false next to each sentence.

_____ 1. Fluorescent bulbs have a glowing filament that produces light.

_____ 2. Electric appliances should be kept far away from water.

_____ 3. Incandescent bulbs produce more heat than fluorescent bulbs.

_____ 4. It is safe to overload an outlet with a lot of plugs.

Circuits

Current electricity needs a path called a circuit. Write **open** or **closed** under each circuit.

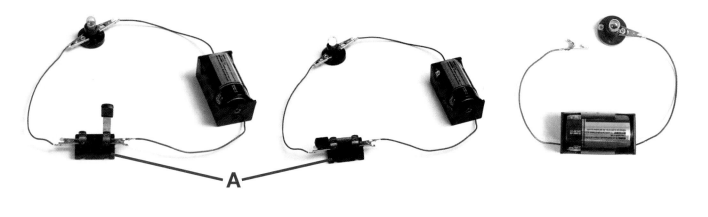

A

_____   _____   _____

What is item **A**?_____

Write **series circuit** or **parallel circuit** under each circuit.

_____   _____

Vocabulary Review

Use the Word Bank to complete the sentences. One word will not be used.

1. The flow of electricity through a conductor is called electric

   _____.

2. The path that electricity can flow through is called a _____.

3. A device that can open or close a circuit is called a _____.

4. A person who designs new technology using electrical energy

   is called an electrical _____.

5. The sudden flow of charged particles from the buildup of

   electric charges on the surface of an object is called

   _____ electricity.

6. The flow of charged particles is called _____.

7. A material that slows down, but does not stop, an electric

   current is called a _____.

8. The flow of electric charges through the air from one object to

   another is called electric _____.

Word Bank		
engineer	static	switch
current	circuit	resistor
discharge	electricity	conductor

My Booklet about Magnets

Name _____

Chapter 7 Vocabulary Words

electromagnet
lines of force
magnet
magnetic field
magnetic pole
magnetism
repel

What does a magnet attract?

Many stories have been written about how magnetism was first discovered. One story tells of people in ancient Greece before the time of Christ. The Greeks discovered unusual black rocks that stuck to each other with a strange force. The rocks also stuck to pieces of iron. Shepherds came home with bits of this strange black rock sticking to the metal tips of their walking sticks. The rocks, called magnetite, were natural magnets.

Another story tells of Chinese people living long ago. The Chinese discovered another interesting property of this strange black rock. They carved rounded pieces of magnetite so that they could rock back and forth. These pieces would turn as they rocked. When they came to rest, they always pointed in the same direction.

Magnetite was discovered by shepherds in the rocky hills of Greece. ▼

People were curious about magnetism, but many years passed before they learned to use it. Magnetite was first used in compasses that helped guide sailing ships across the oceans. Then, in the year 1600, a British scientist named William Gilbert gave an explanation for this curious pointing property of the black rock. He made a hypothesis, and soon other scientists had proved that his hypothesis was correct. Through their investigations, we learned that the earth itself is a magnet, just like the small black rocks that it attracts. Today we know even more about magnets and magnetism.

For centuries, ships relied on compasses to navigate the oceans. ▲

Nuts and bolts made of steel are attracted to magnets.

Magnetism is an invisible force produced by certain objects. This force attracts other objects made of iron or other related metals. Iron is the most familiar magnetic substance. Magnetite is a type of iron. Metals that are made from iron, such as steel, are also magnetic. Many common metals, however, are not magnetic. Aluminum and copper, for example, are not magnetic. Neither are precious metals such as gold and silver. Substances that are not metallic are also not magnetic.

Magnets are metallic objects that attract other objects made of iron, steel, and certain other metals. Magnets have many interesting properties. For instance, if something made of iron or steel touches a magnet, it too becomes a magnet.

Coins are metallic, but are not magnetic. ▲

Sharing Magnetic Force

Place a nail on a donut magnet as shown. With the point of the nail, pick up a second nail.

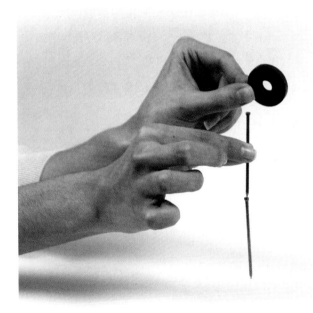

Count to ten, then carefully separate the magnet from the nails. What happens? Try picking up one nail with the other. Are you able? Does one end of the nail work better than the other?

Drop both nails on the table several times. Now try picking up one nail with the other. What has happened?

_____

_____

_____

_____

Magnets link these train cars together.
Why won't some cars connect? ▲

How do magnets repel and attract?

Magnetism is an invisible force found in nature. Magnetic force is found in very large objects, such as our own planet Earth. It is at work in very small particles, such as molecules and atoms, that are the building blocks of all matter. Magnetic force can easily be observed in magnets.

All magnets have two **magnetic poles**. Magnetic force is strongest at a magnet's poles.

You probably know that magnets can behave rather strangely. Magnets can attract each other. But magnets also can repel each other. Repel means to push away. A pole of one magnet will either attract or repel a pole of another magnet.

Each pole of a magnet has a name. One is its north pole. The other is its south pole.

Opposite magnetic poles attract each other. For example, a south pole of one magnet will attract the north pole of another magnet. Magnetic poles that are the same repel each other. A south pole of one magnet will repel the south pole of another magnet. In the same way, the north pole of one magnet will repel the north pole of another magnet. These rules, or physical laws, govern how magnets behave.

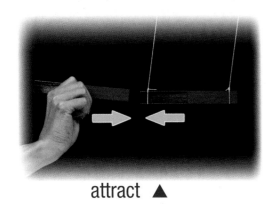

attract ▲

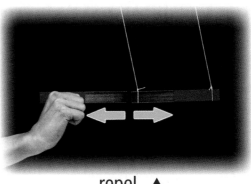

repel ▲

Understanding Polar Attraction

Select a word from the Word Bank to complete each sentence. Some words will not be used.

Word Bank
repel
attract
north
south

1. When two like poles are brought together,

   they _____ each other.

2. The south pole of a magnet will repel the

   _____ pole of another magnet.

Circle the correct word below each pair of magnets.

3. [S   N] [S   N]
   attract / repel

4. [N   S] [N   S]
   attract / repel

5. [N   S] [S   N]
   attract / repel

6. [S   N] [N   S]
   attract / repel

How can you make a magnet?

As you know, all substances are made of atoms. The movement of atoms produces magnetic force.

In a bar of iron, the iron atoms are grouped in small sections. In each section, the atoms act like tiny magnets all pointing in the same direction. However, the sections point in different directions. So the iron bar does not act like a magnet.

A magnet has magnetic force. When an iron bar is stroked with a magnet, the force in the magnet causes atoms in all the sections of the iron bar to line up in the same direction. With all of its sections pointing the same way, the iron bar becomes a magnet with a north and a south pole.

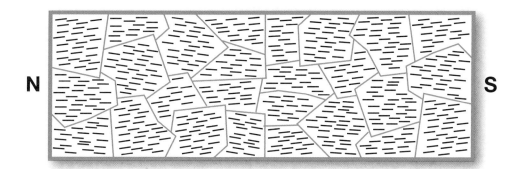

Dropping the iron bar will shake up the sections. The sections will go back to pointing the way they did before, and the iron bar will lose its magnetism.

Electricity in a coil of wire produces a magnetic force. If you place an iron bar inside the coil, the magnetic force of the coil will make the bar act like a magnet. It will remain a magnet as long as the electric current is switched on. This is called an electromagnet. When you switch off the electricity, it won't be a magnet anymore.

Making Magnets

Fill in the circle next to the correct answer.

1. You can make a bar of iron into a magnet by dropping it several times.
   ○ true   ○ false

2. All the sections within a magnet point in the same direction.
   ○ true   ○ false

3. When you stroke a nail with a magnet, the nail will get a north and a south pole.
   ○ true   ○ false

4. Will these two magnets attract or repel?

   | S | N | S | N |

   ○ attract   ○ repel

Imagine the two magnets above joined together into one magnet. Label the poles on the big magnet.

_____ | | _____

What is a magnetic field?

Every magnet is surrounded by an invisible magnetic field in which its force is active. A magnetic field is made of invisible lines of force. Lines of force begin near one of a magnet's poles and travel in loops to the other pole.

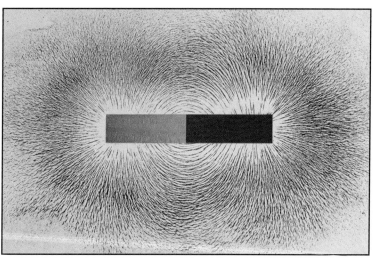

▲ Notice that most of the lines of force traced by these iron filings point to the poles of the bar magnet.

These lines of force cause magnets to attract or repel each other even at a distance. For example, if the south pole of one magnet is brought near the north pole of another magnet, lines of force will stretch from one pole to the other. This will cause the magnets to attract each other.

A light magnetic object, such as a nail or paper clip, is pulled toward a magnet by the lines of force in the magnet's field. As the object gets closer to the magnet's pole, it is attracted with greater force. The force of a magnetic field is strongest at a magnet's poles because most of the lines of force meet there.

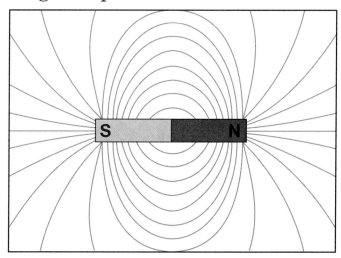

A magnet's power of attraction is greatest at its poles. As the distance from the poles increases, the magnetic field becomes weaker and the magnet's power of attraction becomes less.

Discovering Magnetic Fields

1. Carefully observe the magnetic field of the horseshoe magnet traced by the iron filings in the photograph. Draw lines of force connecting the magnet's poles.

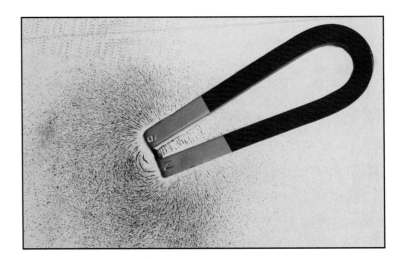

2. Which steel washer is attracted to the magnet with the greatest force?

3.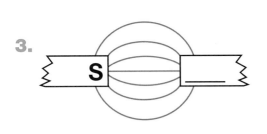

Each drawing below represents the lines of force between two bar magnets. One pole of each pair is labeled. Carefully observe the lines of force in each drawing. Then label the other pole.

3.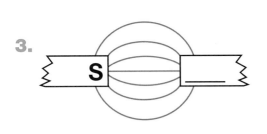

4.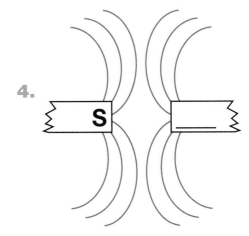

How is the earth like a magnet?

The core of the earth, deep below its surface, is very hot. It contains molten minerals and metals. Scientists believe that the motion of the earth causes molten iron in the earth's core to produce a magnetic field.

Since ancient times, people have noticed the effects of the earth's magnetic field. They used compasses to navigate long before they understood how a compass works.

The earth produces a magnetic field much like a bar magnet, with a north and a south pole. The north-seeking pole of the earth's magnet is located near the true north pole, which is at the very top of the globe. The magnetic south-seeking pole of the earth is located in Antarctica.

◀These hikers carry a compass to help them find their way. When used with a map, a compass can help them pinpoint their location.

A compass needle is a tiny bar magnet. It also has a north and a south pole. The poles of the compass needle are attracted to the magnetic poles of the earth. So the compass needle always points north and south. Using a compass, a sailor can tell if his ship is on course and a hiker can tell which way she is walking.

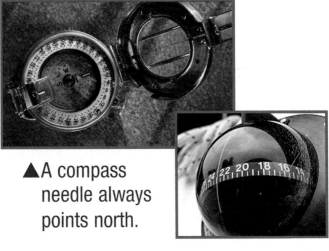

▲A compass needle always points north.

The earth's magnetic field covers a vast area. It reaches from the earth's surface all the way into outer space. In outer space, the earth's magnetic field protects us from cosmic rays and from harmful particles from the sun.

▲This floating, magnetized nail also points north.

Learning About Earth's Magnetic Field

1. Where do scientists think the earth's magnetic field comes from?

_____

2. Why does a compass needle point to the earth's magnetic north pole?

_____

3. List two ways that the earth's magnetic field helps people.

_____

_____

How are magnets used?

Magnets can be found in many places. Think about your house. Are there magnets stuck to the front of your refrigerator holding up notes and pictures? You might not realize it, but there are also magnets inside of your refrigerator. If you open the refrigerator door and hold a paper clip close to the rubber seal around the door, it will stick to it because there is a magnet inside. This magnet is used to keep the door tightly shut.

There are also magnets inside your refrigerator's motor! In fact, there are magnets in almost all electric motors. They can be found in electric mixers, food processors, and can openers. Magnets are also used in telephones and in stereo systems. The speakers in these devices use magnets to make sound.

Maglev trains use magnets. Instead of having wheels that ride on rails, these trains float on magnets! Magnetic repulsion keeps these trains from touching their tracks.

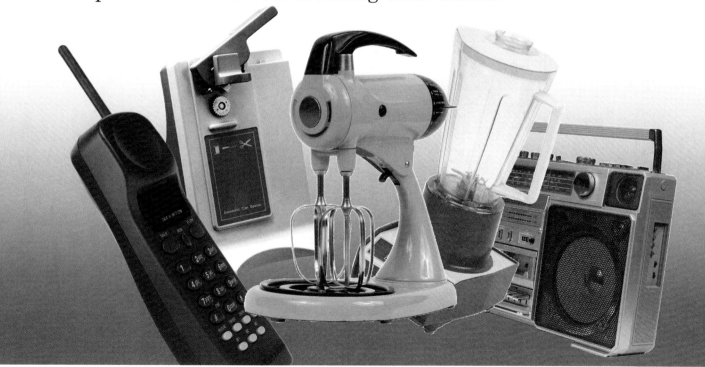

Other Uses of Magnets

At the end of the crane cable is a large electromagnet. It is attracting iron ore. Tell why you think a magnet makes this job easier.

_____

_____

_____

_____

Campers who get lost in the woods can find their way to safety by using a compass. Explain how a compass can be used to help them.

_____

_____

_____

_____

Magnets Review

Like gravity, magnetism is an invisible force that exists as part of God's creation. This mysterious force has been used to help us in many ways. Magnetism keeps notes sticking to your refrigerator, shows hikers the way back to camp, and helps librarians keep track of their library books. And magnets are fun to play with!

Some substances, like iron, are attracted to magnets, or can become magnets themselves. When a magnetic substance becomes a magnet, it has two poles that will attract or repel the poles of other magnets.

Fill in the circle next to the correct answer.

1. | N   S | | S   N |

   ○ attract   ○ repel

2. | N   S | | N   S |

   ○ attract   ○ repel

3. | S   N | | S   N |

   ○ attract   ○ repel

4. | S   N | | N   S |

   ○ attract   ○ repel

5.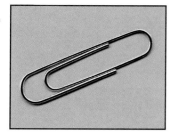

   ○ magnetic

   ○ not magnetic

6.

   ○ magnetic

   ○ not magnetic

7.

   ○ magnetic

   ○ not magnetic

1. The magnets below attract each other.

Show one possible way to label the poles. Show the other way.

2. Label the poles on the two train cars that are repelling each other.

S ___ ___ ___ ___ ___

3. Circle the object that is attracted to the magnet with the greatest force.

N   S

Magnets have many interesting properties. Answer the questions below to see if you remember some of them.

Answer **true** or **false**.

1. A compass detects the lines of force in the earth's magnetic field.   ○ true   ○ false

2. When you stroke a piece of iron with a magnet, the piece of iron will become magnetized.   ○ true   ○ false

3. All magnets have a magnetic field and a north and a south pole.   ○ true   ○ false

4. The north pole of a magnet will repel the south pole of another magnet.   ○ true   ○ false

5. Steel is a substance that can be magnetized.

                                ○ true   ○ false

6. Dropping a magnet may make it lose its magnetism.

                                ○ true   ○ false

Magnets can be very useful. Even the giant magnet inside the earth helps us in several ways.

Fill in the circle of each choice that answers the question correctly. Each question has more than one correct answer.

1. How does the earth's magnetic field help us?
    ○ helps plants grow   ○ shields us from cosmic rays
    ○ helps us tell direction   ○ causes ocean currents

2. Which of these items uses magnets?
    ○ compass   ○ oven
    ○ refrigerator   ○ electric can opener

3. Which of these items produces magnetic fields?
    ○ permanent magnet   ○ Earth
    ○ coal   ○ electrified coil of wire

4. Why does a compass needle turn when a bar magnet is brought near it?

_____

_____

_____

_____

Vocabulary Review

Use the Word Bank to complete the sentences. One word will not be used.

1. A metallic object that attracts other objects made of iron or steel is called a _____.

2. A magnet's force is strongest at its _____.

3. To _____ means to push away.

4. Objects made of iron or related metals are attracted by an invisible force called _____.

5. An _____ is a magnet made from a piece of iron wrapped with a coil of wire through which an electric current is moving.

6. A magnet's force acts in a _____ in the space surrounding the magnet.

7. A magnetic field is made up of _____, which are invisible lines connecting the north and south poles of a magnet.

Word Bank			
repel	lines of force	magnetic field	magnet
magnetism	electromagnet	magnetic poles	attract

My Booklet about
The Musculoskeletal System

Name _____

Chapter 8 Vocabulary Words

ball-and-socket joint
bone marrow
cardiac muscle
compact bone
hinge joint
involuntary movement
joint
ligament
pivot joint
prosthesis
radiologist
skeletal muscles
smooth muscle
spongy bone
tendon
voluntary movement

How do we move?

Basically, we move because our brain tells our body to move. But what are the specific body parts that move? In this chapter we will look at three things that God designed to help us move: bones, joints, and muscles. As you might imagine, there are scientific names for all of your bones. Let's look at a few of them.

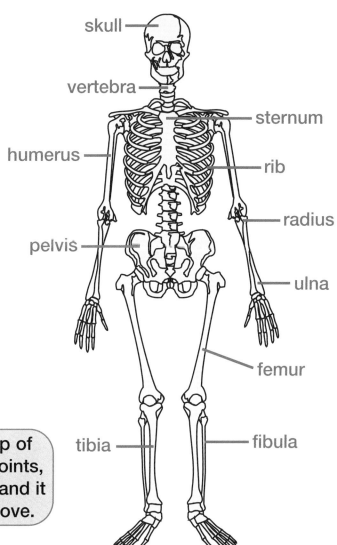

skull
vertebra
sternum
humerus
rib
radius
pelvis
ulna
femur
tibia
fibula

What is the musculoskeletal system?

It is made up of your bones, joints, and muscles and it helps you move.

Did you know that babies are born with over 300 bones in their bodies? By the time they are adults, they only have 206 bones. How could this happen?

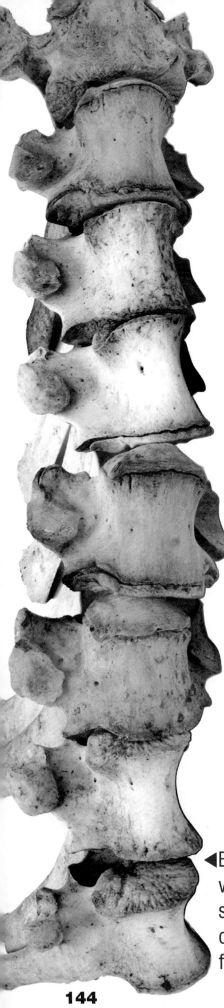

Gently knock on your head. That's your skull. It protects your brain and shapes your face.

Your spine runs down your neck and back. It is made up of 26 bones called vertebrae. They protect your spinal cord and allow you to bend over.

Attached to your spine are your ribs. They form a protective cage around your internal organs. Seven pairs of your ribs attach to the front of your chest on a bone called the sternum. Gently tap the middle of your chest to feel your sternum. You have five other pairs of ribs that only attach to your spine.

◄Bones called vertebrae are stacked on top of each other to form your spine.

▲What bones do you use to throw a baseball?

You have 27 bones in each hand. How many bones are in both hands?

From your shoulder to your elbow is a bone called the humerus. From your elbow to your wrist are two bones called the radius and ulna. These bones allow you to rotate your arm. Stick one arm straight out, palm down. Place your other hand on top of the middle of your forearm. Now turn your palm up. Did you feel your two bones move?

Place your hands on your hips. That's your pelvis. It supports your spinal column and protects the organs in your lower body. Attached to the pelvis is the femur. It is the longest bone in your body and runs from your hip to your knee. Just like the arm, the lower leg contains two bones called the tibia and the fibula.

Be a Radiologist

You may have had an x-ray taken if you have ever broken a bone or gone to the dentist. Radiologists are doctors who look at x-rays and find ways to help people get better. Observe these x-rays. Can you tell which is a hand and which is a foot?

Label each x-ray with **hand** or **foot**.

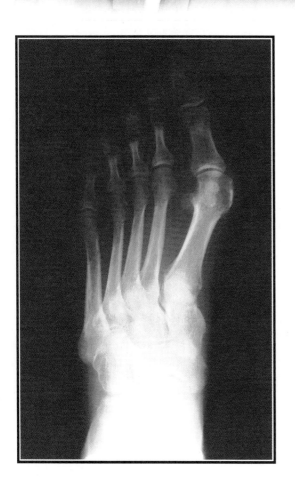

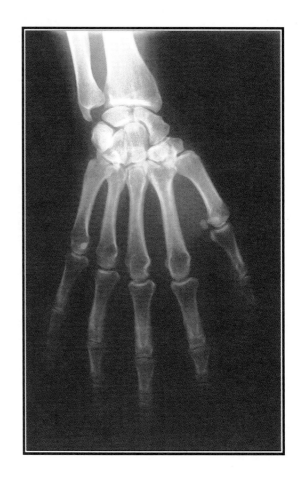

Purposeful Design Science, Level Three • The Musculoskeletal System

What is inside a bone?

When you look at a skeleton, it may seem as if bones are made of one solid, hard, white material. But actually, bones have four different layers.

The first is a thin layer of blood vessels and nerves on the outside of the bone. If you ever break a bone, these nerves send signals to your brain saying, "Ouch! I'm in pain!"

Next is the compact bone. This is the hard, white bone that you are familiar with. It is so strong that surgeons have to use a saw to cut through it! The next layer is spongy bone. Even though its name sounds soft, it is actually quite strong. Spongy bone is designed to bear stress from several directions. It keeps your bones from snapping in half when you bend over or stretch. Within the spaces of the spongy bone is the bone marrow. This is the jelly-like material where blood cells are made.

God designed bones to store calcium and other minerals your body needs. Bones are continually growing and rebuilding themselves. During childhood, your bones are growing the most. You may have noticed that you get taller every year. Eventually, a person's bones stop growing and start breaking down. This is why some older adults get shorter as they grow older.

Can bones heal themselves?

Yes! Bones are designed to repair themselves if they get broken. Cells in your bones work to rebuild the bone just like your skin cells heal when you cut yourself. Casts keep broken bones from moving while they heal. Sometimes doctors use metal plates, screws, and pins to hold bones in place.

Color the Bone

Color the layers of the bone. Label each layer.

Outer layer: blue

Compact bone: green

Spongy bone: yellow

Bone marrow: red

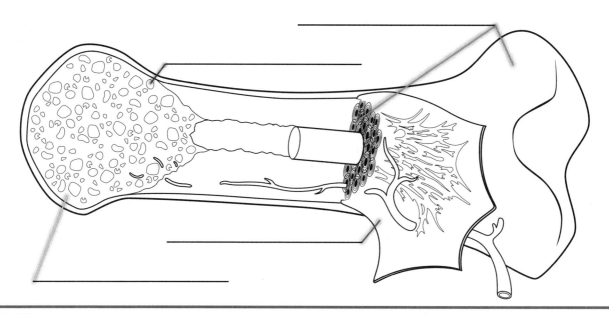

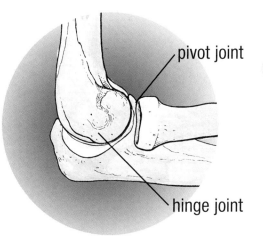

ligament

▲Ligaments connect the bones of your arm.

pivot joint

hinge joint

▲Your elbow has a hinge and a pivot joint.

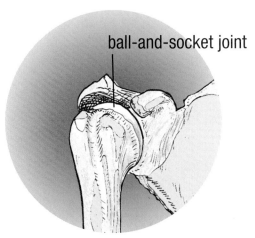

ball-and-socket joint

▲Your shoulder has a ball-and-socket joint.

How are bones connected?

A joint is the connection between two bones. Without joints, your skeleton would be too stiff to move or it would just fall apart and form a big pile of bones! The bones in movable joints are connected by ligaments. These are tough bands of tissue that connect bone to bone.

Bend your knee and then straighten it. Which way did it move? Now bend your pointer finger. How is its movement similar to your knee's? Both joints are hinge joints. They move back and forth like the hinges on a door. What about your elbow? Does it move the same way as the knee and the finger? Try it. You probably noticed that it does move back and forth like your knee, but it can also be pivoted so that your palm faces up and then down.

The elbow joint is a combination of a hinge and a pivot joint. Pivot joints allow bones to turn. Look left! Now look right! You just moved a true pivot joint at the top of your spine between the top two vertebrae. It allows your head to turn from side to side.

Swing your arm around in a circle. The joint in your shoulder is called a ball-and-socket joint. You also have one in each hip. Ball-and-socket joints allow movement in all directions. They are called ball-and-socket joints because the rounded end of one bone fits into a cup-shaped part on another bone.

Circle the Joints

Look at the skeleton. Circle a hinge joint, a pivot joint, and a ball-and-socket joint. Draw a line from each joint to the word that describes it.

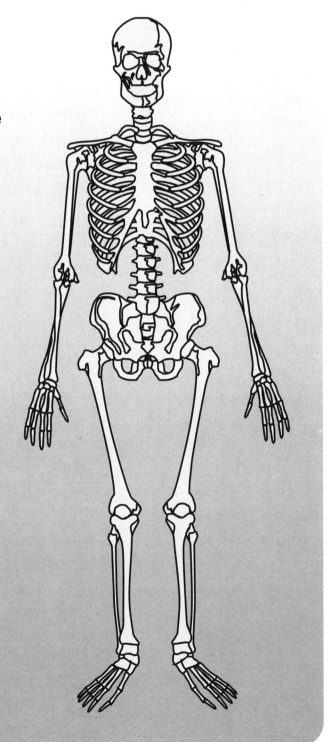

hinge joint

pivot joint

ball-and-socket joint

How do muscles help us move?

Pick up a book and hold it over your head. How did you do that? Using your bones, joints, and muscles, you were able to pick up that book and then put it down. Your body has over 600 muscles. Most of these are skeletal muscles which are attached to your bones. The movements you make with them are called voluntary movements because you can control them.

Skeletal muscles are attached to bones with tendons. This tough tissue connects the muscles firmly to the bones. Muscles can only pull, not push, so they often work in pairs. Look at your arm, for example. To raise your forearm, your biceps muscle contracts or bunches up. You can feel this if you place

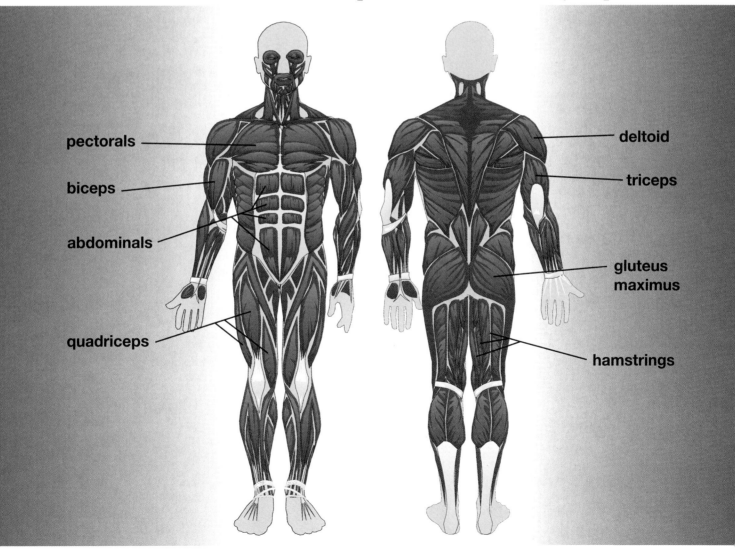

pectorals

biceps

abdominals

quadriceps

deltoid

triceps

gluteus maximus

hamstrings

your hand on top of it and raise your arm. At the same time, your triceps muscle on the back of your upper arm relaxes or stretches out. When you lower your arm, your triceps muscle contracts and your biceps muscle relaxes.

Do you know the name of the muscles of your chest? They are called pectorals. You may have heard body builders refer to them as their "pecs." Sometimes you hear people saying they really need to do sit-ups to strengthen their "abs." They are referring to their abdominal muscles. Your abdominal muscles act as a support for your internal organs. They also assist you in bending over and sideways.

Name that muscle!

These muscles are found on your shoulders.	If you are sitting down, you are sitting on these muscles right now!
_____	_____
These muscles are found on the front of your upper legs.	These muscles are found on the back of your upper legs.
_____	_____

Draw an arrow to show how each muscle pulls the bones.

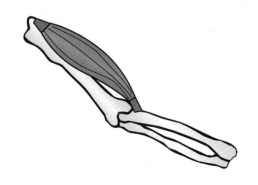 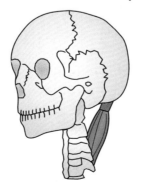 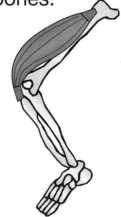

Are there muscles that don't move bones?

When you think of muscles, you probably think of the ones that move your bones. But did you know that some muscles move other parts of your body? For example, your stomach and intestines have a kind of muscle called smooth muscle. When these smooth muscles contract, they move food through your digestive system. Your heart has another type of muscle called cardiac muscle. The contractions of cardiac muscles pump blood through your heart. Smooth muscles and cardiac muscle produce involuntary movements. These are movements that you do not consciously control. Your brain tells these muscles to move and they do it without you even being aware of it.

Most skeletal muscles move bones. But some skeletal muscles produce voluntary movements in your face, even though they do not move bones! What do they move? Move your eyes around. How did you do that? You have several muscles that work together to move your eyeballs. You can move your eyes up, down, and sideways by moving your eye muscles. One end of each muscle is attached to the top, bottom, or side of the eyeball. The other ends are attached to the bone in the eye socket.

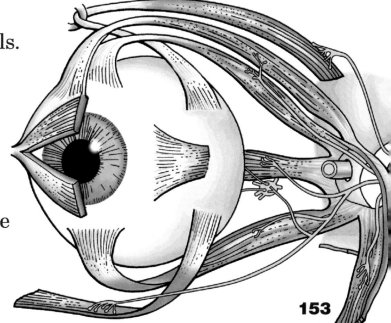

You also have muscles that move different parts of your face. The muscles in your face attach to the underside of your skin. You can control these muscles to make different expressions and communicate a variety of emotions.

Let's Face It

Look at the boy's face and color in the muscle he is using.

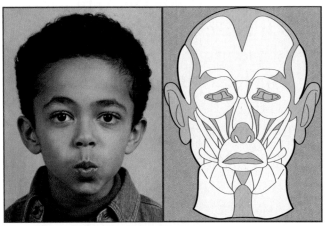

The orbicularis oris encircles your mouth. It allows you to push your lips forward.

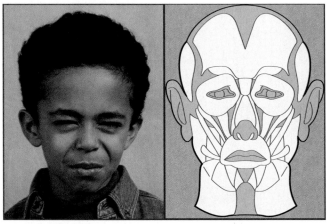

The orbicularis occuli encircles your eye. It allows you to squint.

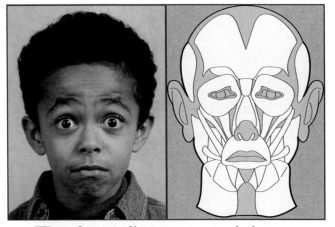

The frontalis runs straight up across your forehead above your eye. It allows you to raise your eyebrows.

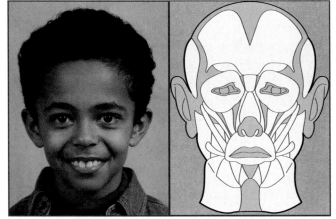

The zygomaticus major runs diagonally from the corner of your lips up the side of your cheek. It allows you to smile.

Look in a mirror and make some other expressions. Try to identify which muscles you are using to move your face.

What is a prosthesis?

What would happen if you lost an arm or a leg in an accident? You would most likely be fitted with an artificial limb called a prosthesis. You've probably seen cartoons that have pirates with wooden legs and hooks for hands. A long time ago, that is what people who lost their legs and arms had to do. They would make artificial limbs out of wood or metal to replace the ones lost due to injury or illness.

Over time, scientists and doctors developed better and better ways to make prosthetic limbs. Soon they were making ones that had movable joints. A famous German knight, Götz von Berlichingen, had an artificial hand built with jointed fingers. He could hold a sword with this artificial hand.

Nowadays, prosthetic limbs have improved quite significantly. With modern technology, doctors are able to make artificial body parts that look and move a lot like the real thing. Some are so lifelike that you would not even know someone had a prosthesis unless he or she told you. Scientists have even developed ways to replace injured body parts besides arms and legs.

How Do Prosthetics Help People?

Scientists have developed artificial arms and legs to help people. They also have developed other artificial body parts. These parts help people who have been injured or whose bodies are just getting older. Many times as adults get older, body parts stop working properly. Read about each prosthetic and write how it helps each person.

Tatiana's heart stopped working properly, so doctors replaced some of her heart valves with artificial ones. Now it can pump blood through her body again. How did this prosthesis improve her life?

_____

_____

Jamal lost his left eye in an accident. Doctors replaced his damaged eye with an artificial one. He can't see with it, but it looks and moves like his right eye. How did this prosthesis improve his life?

_____

_____

Carson was a soccer player. After years of running and kicking the ball, his knee was damaged. So, he had surgery and the doctors replaced his knee joint with a metal one. How did this prosthesis improve his life?

_____

_____

Musculoskeletal Review

Your bones, joints, and muscles all help you move. Let's review what you learned during this chapter!

Muscles can only pull, not push. Draw an arrow to show the direction the muscle will pull the bone.

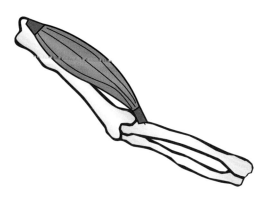
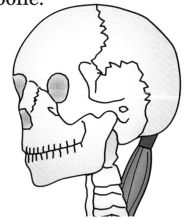

Read the sentences. Write the number next to the layer each sentence describes.

1. Spongy bone looks like a sponge and is found deeper inside the bone.

2. Compact bone is the smooth, hard, white layer of bone.

3. Bone marrow is a jelly-like material that makes red blood cells and is located within the spaces of the spongy bone.

4. There is a thin layer of blood vessels and nerves on the outside of the bone.

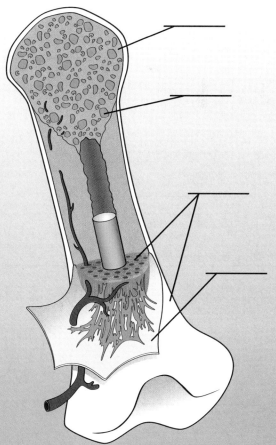

Use the words from the Word Bank or the drawing to complete the sentences.

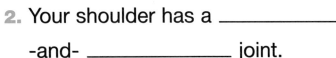

Word Bank		
ball-and-socket	pivot	hinge

1. Your _____ protects your brain.

2. Your shoulder has a _____ -and- _____ joint.

3. Your _____ muscle pulls your forearm up.

4. Your _____ protect your internal organs.

5. Your knee has a _____ joint.

6. Your _____ muscles are found in your chest.

7. Your neck has a _____ joint.

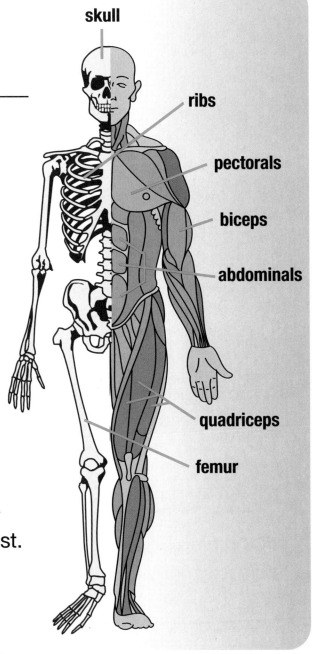

skull

ribs

pectorals

biceps

abdominals

quadriceps

femur

Where are these muscles found?
Draw a line from the words to the pictures.

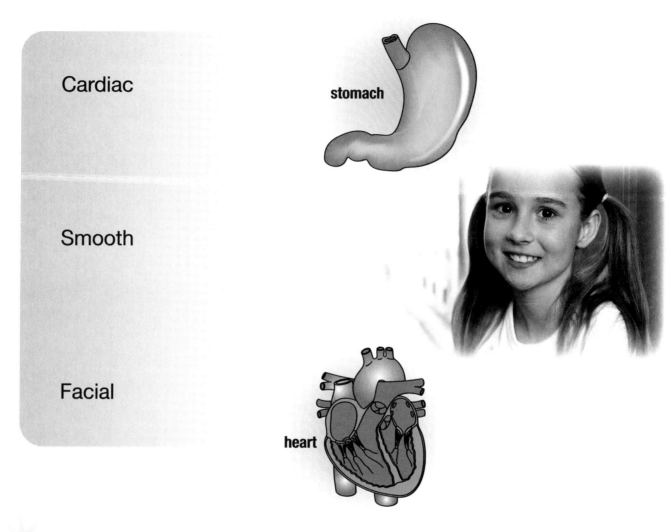

Cardiac

stomach

Smooth

Facial

heart

Think about it:

How do artificial body parts improve people's lives? Write about a specific example.

_____

_____

_____

_____

Vocabulary Review

Use the Word Bank to complete the sentences. One word will not be used.

1. A _____ is the connection between two bones.

2. A _____ is an artificial body part.

3. A _____ is a doctor who looks at x-rays and finds ways to help people get better.

4. Tough bands of tissue that connect bone to bone are called

   _____ .

5. Movements that a person does not consciously control are called

   _____ .

6. Muscles that are attached to bones and produce voluntary movements are called

   _____ .

7. Movements a person can control are called

   _____ .

8. The strong, connective tissues that bind muscles to bones are called

   _____ .

My Booklet about The Nervous System

Name _____

Chapter 9 Vocabulary Words

autonomic nervous system
brain stem
cerebellum
cerebrum
left hemisphere
motor nerve
neurologist
right hemisphere
sensory nerve

How do you know when to duck?

You are sitting in the bleachers watching a baseball game. Suddenly, a ball comes flying straight towards your head! You cover your head with your hands and duck just as the ball goes sailing over you. That was close! How did your body know what to do to keep you safe? It knew because of your nervous system.

▲ Your nervous system allows you to swing a bat, run to first base, and duck out of the way if a ball comes flying toward you!

Your nervous system controls your entire body. The nervous system receives information about the world around you through your senses. It then processes this information and tells your body how to react. It also controls things you aren't usually aware of, like your body temperature, your heartbeat, and your breathing.

◀ Your nervous system is always working, even when you aren't thinking about it!

The Nervous System

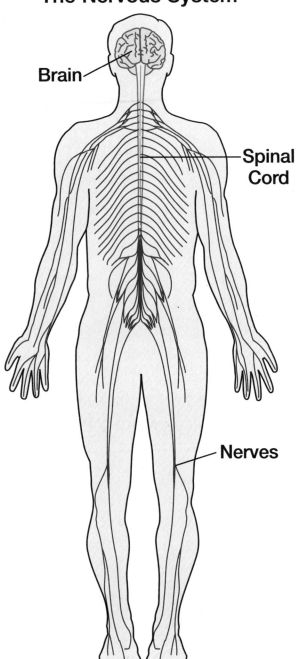

Brain

Spinal Cord

Nerves

God designed the nervous system with three basic parts. First there is the brain. It is the control center. It tells your body what to do. Next is the spinal cord. It extends from the base of your brain down the middle of your back. It is protected by your vertebral column.

What's a neurologist?
A neurologist is a doctor who treats disorders of the nervous system. This includes diseases of the brain, spinal cord, and nerves. Can you guess what a *neurosurgeon* does? What about a *neuroradiologist*?

Finally, God put together an intricate network of nerves that reaches to all areas of your body. Nerves connect to the brain and spinal cord and branch out over the entire body. They are like telephone wires in a city. Nerves provide a way for the brain to communicate with all the parts of the body. If something happens to your right big toe, nerves send the message to the brain. The brain processes this information and then sends a message down to your toe to tell it how to react.

Nerves carry messages through your body, kind of like telephone wires carry messages from city to city. ▶

▲Your nervous system allows you to bend your legs, decide which color to use, hold a crayon, and talk with your friends.

Trace the Pathway

Your nervous system takes in information through your senses. After it processes sensory information, it sends a message to different body parts telling them how to react. All of this is done almost instantly! So if you step on a piece of broken glass, your brain recognizes pain and danger and tells your leg to lift your foot off of the glass very quickly.

Lucy's nervous system alerted her to a fire in her kitchen. It also helped her get out of the house safely. Draw red arrows from the sentence to her brain showing information going to her brain. Draw blue arrows from her brain to the sentence showing information coming out of her brain.

1. She smells smoke.

2. She hears a crackling noise.

3. She feels the fire's warmth on her face.

4. She sees the flames.

5. She yells for help.

6. She runs outside.

7. She calls the fire department.

What is your "funny nerve"?

Have you ever bumped your elbow and felt a tingly, numbing sensation? Someone may have told you, "Oh, you bumped your funny bone." But your funny bone is not a bone at all, it is actually a nerve! It's called the ulnar nerve. (Do you remember the bone in your forearm called the ulna?) When you bump your arm on something, this nerve presses against your humerus and you feel a strange sensation.

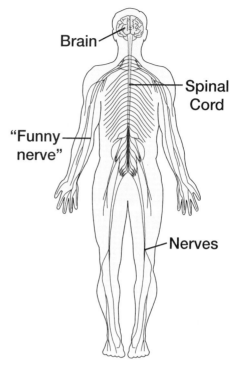

Brain

Spinal Cord

"Funny nerve"

Nerves

A huge network of nerves runs throughout your body. These nerves carry messages between your brain and all your body parts. Sensory nerves carry information from your body parts to the brain. Motor nerves carry information from the brain to other body parts.

◄ Sensory nerves carry information from your eyes to your brain. Motor nerves carry messages to your hand when it is time to turn the page.

You have nerves in every part of your body. There are nerves in your nose that help you smell. There are nerves in all your muscles that tell them to move. There are even nerves in your face that make your tear glands produce tears.

◀ Nerves in your face cause your tear glands to produce tears when you cry.

What happens when I stub my toe?

You stubbed your toe. Fill in the circle next to the type of nerve carrying the message.

1. Nerves carry messages of pain from your toe to your brain.
   ○ sensory   ○ motor

2. Nerves carry messages to your muscles telling them to raise your leg and hold your foot with your hands.
   ○ sensory   ○ motor

3. Nerves carry messages from your brain to your leg muscles and tell you to hop up and down.
   ○ sensory   ○ motor

4. After about 30 seconds, nerves carry messages from your toe to your brain that say the pain is gone.
   ○ sensory   ○ motor

Who's in charge?

Your brain, that's who! It allows you to move, breathe, think, speak, see, smell, hear, and even sleep. In fact, everything that you do is controlled by your brain.

When you imagine what a brain looks like, you might think it is a big, wrinkly blob. But it actually has specific parts. Each part has its own function.

The largest part is the **cerebrum**. It is the part that enables you to think. You use it to do math, read a book, and remember how to tie your shoes. The cerebrum also controls the muscles that produce voluntary movements.

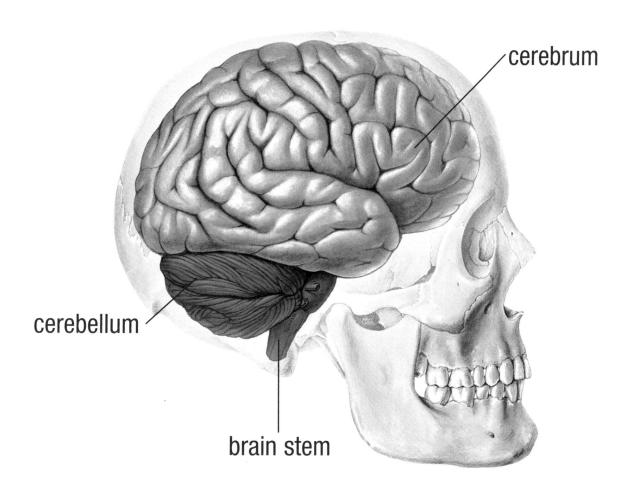

cerebrum

cerebellum

brain stem

Below the cerebrum, is the cerebellum. It looks tiny, but it does a lot. It controls your balance, movement, and coordination. The next time you ride your bike, remember that it's your cerebellum that keeps you balanced and moving in the right direction.

Beneath the cerebellum is the brain stem. It connects the rest of your brain to your spinal cord. The brain stem controls your involuntary muscles. These are the muscles that work without you even thinking about it. It helps your lungs breathe air, your stomach digest food, and your heart beat quickly or slowly.

What does each brain part do?

Draw a line from the words to the part of the brain responsible for each action.

running

speaking

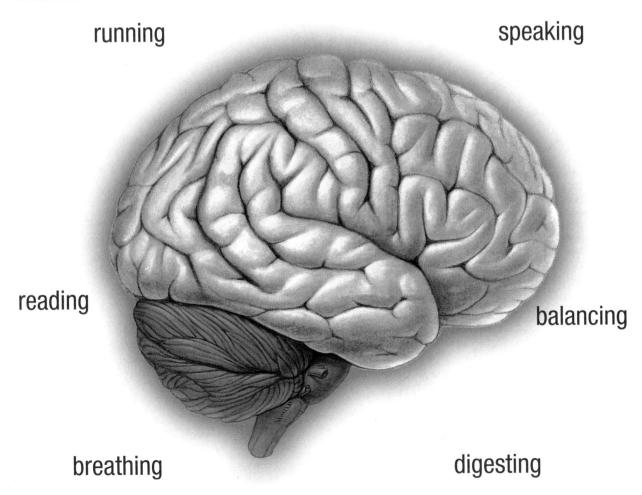

reading

balancing

breathing

digesting

What else does your brain do?

Do you write with your left or right hand? Do you kick a soccer ball with your left or right foot? Which side of your brain controls your left hand? your right? You might be surprised to learn that the right side of your brain controls your left hand and the left side of your brain controls your right hand!

Your cerebrum is divided into two parts called hemispheres. The left hemisphere controls the right side of the body. The right hemisphere controls the left side of the body.

Each hemisphere has different areas that do different things. The area near your forehead controls learning. You use this area a lot in school. At the back of the cerebrum is the area that controls vision. One area of the cerebrum controls memory.

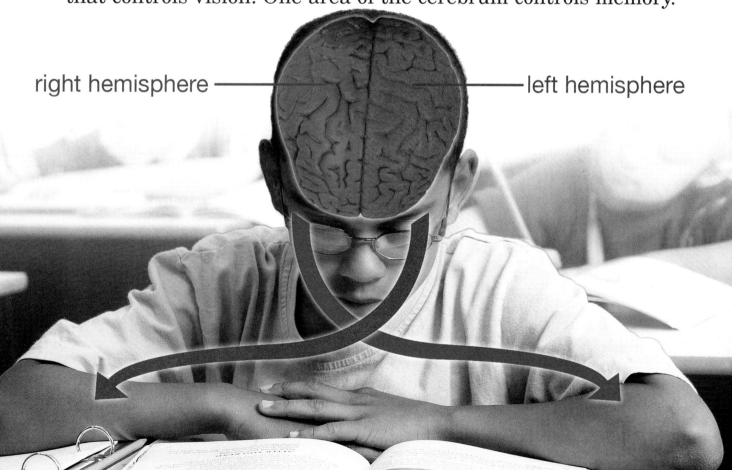

right hemisphere ——————————— ————left hemisphere

Did you know that you have different kinds of memory? One is called long-term memory. It stores everything you know. You can keep filling it up throughout your life and it will never get full!

Your long-term memory stores things like your best friend's name, how to brush your teeth, and who won the World Series last year. Can you think of any other things that would be stored in your long-term memory?

On the other hand, your short-term memory can only store a small amount of information for a short amount of time. Every few minutes, facts in your short-term memory are replaced by new information. The old information either moves to your long-term memory or is forgotten.

Test Your Short-Term Memory

Your short-term memory can only store about seven things at one time. Try it. Have someone read this list of numbers to you. Try to write down as many as you can in the right order. Most people can only remember between five and seven numbers.

5-3-7-2-8-5-1-9-4-5-0-7

What controls your heartbeat?

Have you ever been sitting quietly, when someone walked up behind you and scared you? Did you notice that your heart started beating quickly? You didn't think about increasing your heartbeat, but it happened just the same.

These actions that you cannot control are called involuntary actions. A special part of your nervous system is in charge of all the involuntary actions of your body. It is called the autonomic nervous system.

Your body is constantly trying to maintain a state of balance. Your autonomic nervous system helps it do that. For example, if you are in danger, your autonomic nervous system will increase your heart rate. Once you reach safety, your autonomic nervous system will decrease your heart rate.

The autonomic nervous system can have two different effects on the body parts it controls. For example, it can cause your pupils to get larger or get smaller. It can make your heart beat faster or slower. It can even make your mouth produce more saliva or dry it up!

◄Your autonomic nervous system slows down your heart as you sleep.

What is your body doing?

Read each situation. How does your autonomic nervous system affect each body part?

You are walking along the beach at sunset. It is getting darker and darker. What are your pupils doing?

    O getting smaller   O getting larger

You are lying in bed and the lights are off. Your little brother turns the lights on suddenly. What are your pupils doing?

    O getting smaller   O getting larger

You are running around the playground at recess. What is your heart rate doing?

    O decreasing   O increasing

You are nervous about the big soccer game this afternoon. What does your mouth do?

    O dries up   O produces more saliva

You are about to eat your favorite food. What does you mouth do?

    O dries up   O produces more saliva

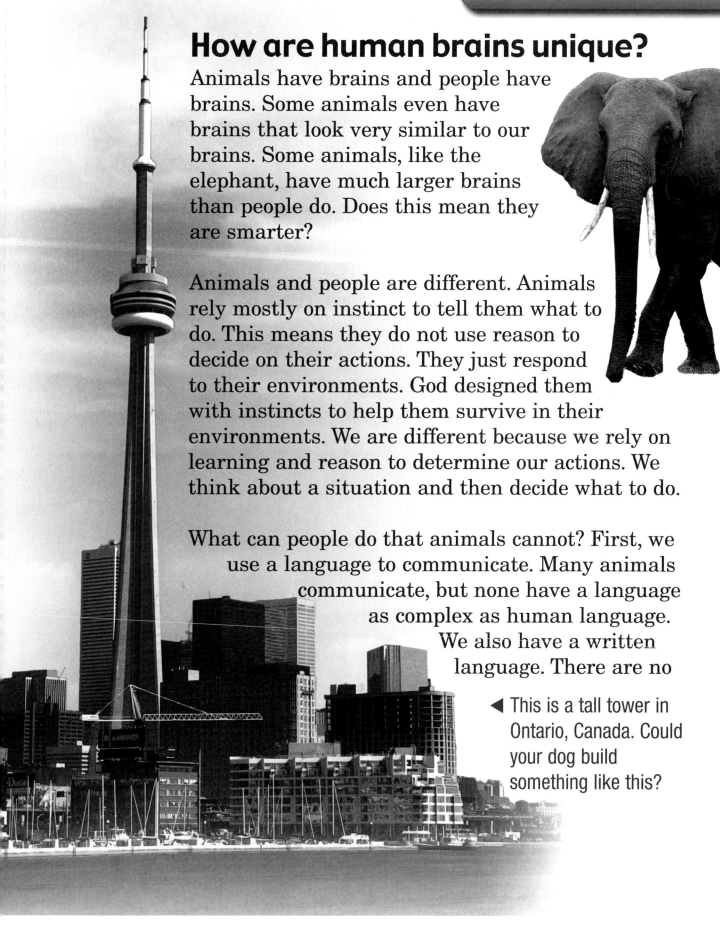

How are human brains unique?

Animals have brains and people have brains. Some animals even have brains that look very similar to our brains. Some animals, like the elephant, have much larger brains than people do. Does this mean they are smarter?

Animals and people are different. Animals rely mostly on instinct to tell them what to do. This means they do not use reason to decide on their actions. They just respond to their environments. God designed them with instincts to help them survive in their environments. We are different because we rely on learning and reason to determine our actions. We think about a situation and then decide what to do.

What can people do that animals cannot? First, we use a language to communicate. Many animals communicate, but none have a language as complex as human language. We also have a written language. There are no

◀ This is a tall tower in Ontario, Canada. Could your dog build something like this?

Claude Monet, a famous artist, painted this masterpiece. ▲

great animal authors! An animal cannot write a novel or even the simple directions on the back of a shampoo bottle.

Our brains have the unique ability to foresee the consequences of our actions. We can think about situations and then make decisions. We can exercise self-control over our actions. Animals cannot. We also know the difference between right and wrong and good and evil. God made us special in this way.

People have used their brains to study science, develop technology, and create art and music. What are some other things that people can do that animals cannot do?

How are we different?

Draw a line from the sentence to the animal or person it describes.

I rely on my instincts to tell me when to eat.

I think before I make decisions.

I can read and write.

I rely on my instincts to tell me when to sleep.

I can plan what I am going to do.

I know the difference between right and wrong.

The Nervous System Review

Your nervous system controls all voluntary and involuntary actions of your body. It helps you move, think, sleep, and stay alive! Let's review what you learned in this chapter.

Use the Word Bank to label the three parts of the nervous system. Some words will not be used.

Word Bank
brain
nerves
blood vessels
spinal cord
backbone

_____

_____

_____

Read the sentences. Write **S** if the sentence is describing the function of a sensory nerve. Write **M** if the sentence is describing the function of a motor nerve.

_____ 1. Your nose smells freshly-baked cookies. Nerves carry this information to the brain.

_____ 2. Your eyes see the cookies on the kitchen counter. Nerves carry this information to the brain.

_____ 3. Nerves carry information from your brain to your legs and you walk towards the cookies.

_____ 4. Nerves carry information from your brain to your hand. You pick up a cookie and take a bite.

_____ 5. The cookie tastes delicious. Nerves carry this information from your mouth to your brain.

Some body parts are more sensitive to touch than others. Look at the girl. Note the body parts labeled.

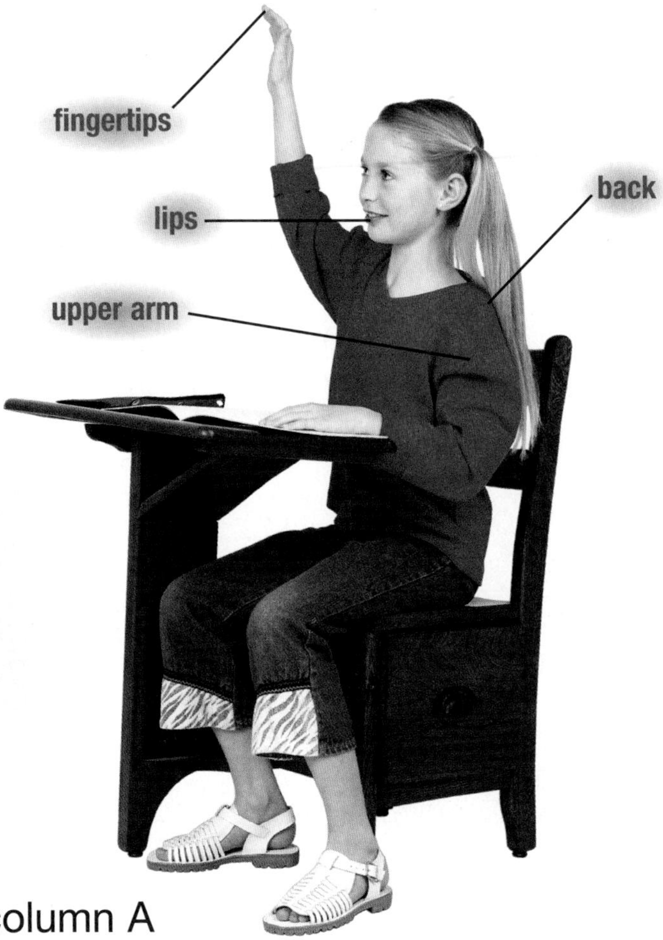

fingertips

lips

back

upper arm

Circle the two most sensitive body parts. Draw a square around the two least sensitive body parts.

Draw a line from the word in column A to its description in column B.

A

cerebrum •

cerebellum •

brain stem •

right hemisphere •

left hemisphere •

B

• controls left side of body

• controls involuntary muscles that work to keep your body alive

• controls balance, movement, and coordination

• controls right side of body

• controls thinking and voluntary movements

Use the Word Bank to label the three parts
of the brain.

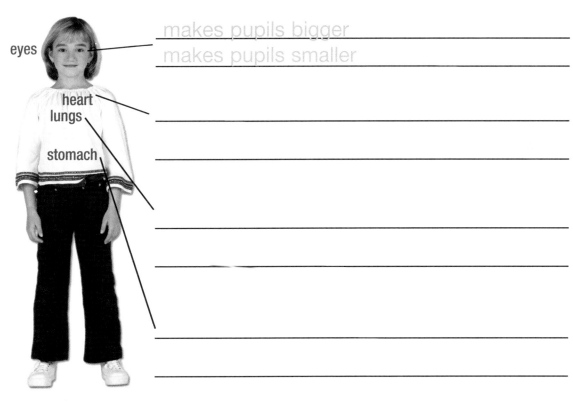

Word Bank

brain stem
cerebrum
cerebellum

Your autonomic nervous system can either speed up or slow down
your body's functions. Write two things the autonomic nervous
system can do to each organ. The first one has been done for you.

eyes _makes pupils bigger_
makes pupils smaller

heart
lungs _____

stomach _____

_____

_____

_____

List three things that your brain can do that an animal's brain
cannot.

1. _____

2. _____

3. _____

Vocabulary Review

Use the Word Bank to complete the sentences.

Word Bank			
neurologist	sensory	motor	left
cerebrum	cerebellum	stem	autonomic
right			

1. The brain's _____ hemisphere generally controls the left side of the body.

2. The _____ is located below the cerebrum. It controls balance, movement, and coordination.

3. A doctor who treats disorders of the nervous system is called a _____.

4. Nerves that carry information from the brain to other body parts are called _____ nerves.

5. The brain _____ connects the brain to the spinal cord. It controls involuntary muscles that work to keep your body alive.

6. The _____ is the largest part of the brain. It controls thinking and voluntary movements.

7. The brain's _____ hemisphere generally controls the right side of the body.

8. Nerves that carry information from the body parts to the brain are called _____ nerves.

9. The _____ nervous system controls all involuntary actions of the body.

My Booklet about Health

Name _____

Chapter 10 Vocabulary Words

carbohydrate
diet
fat
habit
mineral
nutrient
nutritionist
protein
vitamin

How can you stay healthy and live well?

God designed your body to grow and change throughout your lifetime. You began life as a baby, became a toddler, and now are a child. In a few years, you will become a teenager and then an adult. What does your body need in order to function properly as you move through each stage in your life cycle?

What can you do to keep your body healthy and well?

People need several things to help them stay healthy and live well. One thing we need is food. Our bodies need food for energy. Can you eat just any kind of food you want and be healthy? No, the kind of food you eat is important. Some foods are better for you than other foods.

What kinds of foods do you usually eat?

We also need water to keep all our organs and body systems working properly. About 65 percent of the human body is made of water. That is a lot of water! It is important to make sure your body gets enough water every day.

How much water do you drink every day?

Our bodies also need to get adequate amounts of sleep to stay healthy. Without enough sleep, your body cannot perform its normal tasks as well.

How much sleep do you usually get every night?

Exercise is very important to staying healthy. It helps keep your bones, joints, and muscles working properly.

How much exercise do you usually do every week?

Your Health Habits

Think about your current health habits. Answer the questions.

1. List everything you ate yesterday.

   Breakfast:_____

   _____

   Lunch:_____

   _____

   Dinner:_____

   _____

   Snacks:_____

   _____

2. How many glasses of water did you drink yesterday?

   _____

3. How many hours did you sleep last night?

   _____

4. What kind of exercise did you do yesterday?

   _____

   How long did you exercise?

   _____

What is a nutritionist?
A nutritionist is a person who plans food programs and diets. He or she talks with people to evaluate their current health. Then the nutritionist offers recommendations on how to change their diets to include healthier food choices. Nutritionists work to help people stay healthy.

Does what you eat really matter?

Could you survive on a diet of just potato chips? What if you only ate oranges and nothing else? You probably know that potato chips aren't the healthiest food choice, but oranges are healthy! Does that mean it is all right to just eat oranges? Oranges are good for you, but they don't contain all the nutrients your body needs.

So what are nutrients, anyway? Nutrients are substances in food that keep the body working properly. Water is a nutrient. Did you know that a person can survive months without food, but only 8 to 10 days without water? Your body needs water to keep all of your organs and systems working properly. You can drink water in a glass. You can also get some of the water you need from foods. Grapes, watermelon, and cucumbers have a lot of water in them. Can you think of any other foods that contain a lot of water?

Other nutrients your body needs are carbohydrates, proteins, and fats. You can get these from eating a variety of foods. Each nutrient has a specific function in your body. It is important to remember that your body needs foods that contain all four of these nutrients every day.

A carbohydrate is the nutrient that provides the biggest energy source for your body. Examples of foods that contain carbohydrates are pasta, breads and cereals, potatoes, and fruits.

A protein is the nutrient that helps build and repair your body tissues. Examples of foods that contain proteins are dairy products, meats, beans, nuts, and whole grains.

A fat is the nutrient that provides a concentrated energy source for your body. Examples of foods that contain fats are eggs, dairy products, meats, avocados, some nuts, and oils.

What are you eating?

Look at the meal below. How does this meal provide the following nutrients? Write the foods that provide the nutrients.

Water _____

_____

Carbohydrates _____

_____

Proteins _____

_____

Fats _____

_____

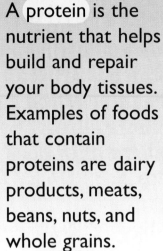

Do I really need to eat my vegetables?

Your parents were right! Vegetables and fruits are good for you because they contain nutrients called vitamins and minerals. Vitamins are substances in food that help your body stay healthy and work properly. Minerals are non-living, natural substances found in the earth. In foods, they also help keep your body healthy and working properly.

Vitamin	Function	Sources
A	Helps eyesight, skin, bones, teeth, and gums	Carrots, sweet potatoes, dark-green leafy vegetables, milk
B group (B_1, B_2, B_3, B_6, B_{12}, and folic acid)	Helps your body make energy and red blood cells	Whole grains, meat, poultry, fish, eggs, dark-green leafy vegetables
C	Helps form healthy skin, teeth, tendons, bones; helps wounds to heal	Oranges, grapefruit, strawberries, broccoli, tomatoes
D	Helps bones, cartilage, and teeth	Fortified milk, salmon, tuna, egg yolks
E	Helps your blood carry oxygen through the body	Whole grains, dark-green leafy vegetables, nuts
K	Helps your blood to clot	Dark-green leafy vegetables

Mineral	Function	Sources
Iron	Helps blood carry oxygen through the body	Meat, eggs, nuts, dried beans, dark-green leafy vegetables
Calcium	Helps build strong teeth and bones	Dairy products, dark-green leafy vegetables, broccoli, salmon
Potassium	Helps keep muscles and nervous system working well	Bananas, beans, whole grains, oranges, tomatoes, broccoli
Zinc	Helps your body fight infection and illness; helps wounds heal	Meat, milk, whole grains, nuts, eggs

Identify Sources of Vitamins and Minerals

Name a food that is a good source of each of the following vitamins and minerals. Tell how each helps your body.

	Food Source	How it helps your body
Vitamin C	_____	_____
		_____
Vitamin A	_____	_____
		_____
Vitamin D	_____	_____
		_____
Calcium	_____	_____
		_____
Iron	_____	_____
		_____

What is a diet?

When you hear the word "diet" you might think it is just something adults do when they are trying to lose weight. But diet does not just refer to weight-loss plans. The word **diet** refers to all the food you eat, whether healthy or unhealthy. So what is a healthy diet? A healthy diet is a varied diet. That means that you eat a lot of different kinds of foods. You need to eat foods that include all of the six nutrients: fats, carbohydrates, proteins, vitamins, minerals, and water.

The MyPyramid Food Guidance System suggests guidelines for health. The person going up the stairs on the left side of the pyramid represents the need for a balance between the amount of food you eat and the amount of physical activity you get every day. If you eat more food (energy) than you use in one day, you will gain weight. If you don't eat enough food (energy) to match your physical activity level, you will lose weight. It is important to find the right balance for you between food and physical activity.

MyPyramid.gov
STEPS TO A HEALTHIER YOU

The MyPyramid Food Guidance System gives guidelines of how much of each kind of food you need every day. The amount you need depends on how much energy you need each day. Each food group is represented by a different color band. The widths of the bands suggest how much food you need from each group.

MyPyramid
STEPS TO A HEALTHIER YOU
MyPyramid.gov

GRAINS	VEGETABLES	FRUITS	MILK	MEAT & BEANS
You should eat between 5 and 6 ounces of grains a day. At least half of those ounces should come from whole grains. One ounce equals about one slice of bread, one cup of dry cereal, or $\frac{1}{2}$ cup of rice or pasta.	You should eat between 2 and $2\frac{1}{2}$ cups of vegetables a day. Try to eat a variety of vegetables such as dark-green, orange, starchy, dry beans and peas, and other vegetables every week.	You should eat $1\frac{1}{2}$ cups of fruits a day. It is best to make most choices fruits, not juices. It is also important to vary the kinds of fruits you eat.	You should eat about 3 cups of low-fat or fat-free foods from this group every day. Cheese and yogurt are also part of this group. One cup equals a slice of cheese or a glass of milk.	You should eat 5 ounces of low-fat foods from this group every day. One ounce equals 1 tablespoon of peanut butter, $\frac{1}{2}$ ounce of nuts, or $\frac{1}{4}$ cups of dry beans.

The yellow band represents oils. You need about five teaspoons of oils a day. Oils are found in many foods such as baked goods and salad dressings. You should limit the amount of extra fats and sugars in your diet.

Do you get enough sleep and exercise?

How much sleep do you get every night? The amount of sleep a person needs is different for everyone, but most kids your age need between 10 and 11 hours of sleep every night. Sleep is a very important and necessary part of your health. It allows your body to rest and get ready for the next day. If you don't get enough sleep, you feel cranky and clumsy. Your brain is not able to think or work as quickly. When you don't get enough sleep, it is very hard to concentrate in school.

Another important part of your health is exercise. Your body needs exercise to keep working properly. Exercise helps keep your bones, muscles, and joints strong. It strengthens your heart, improves your posture, allows you to sleep better at night, and helps your body fight illnesses better. It also keeps you at a healthy weight. Exercise can even make you feel happy and put you in a good mood!

The great thing about exercise is that you can do it anywhere! Playing on the playground, jumping rope in your driveway, and playing catch with a friend are all ways you can exercise. Can you think of any other ways to exercise?

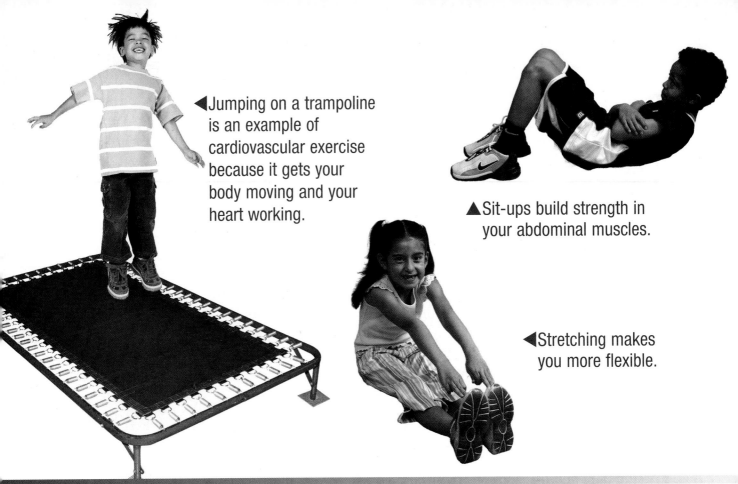

◀Jumping on a trampoline is an example of cardiovascular exercise because it gets your body moving and your heart working.

▲Sit-ups build strength in your abdominal muscles.

◀Stretching makes you more flexible.

Three Kinds of Exercise

There are three kinds of exercise that you should do regularly to keep your body healthy.

Exercise	Examples	Other examples
Cardiovascular: This kind of exercise gets your body moving and your heart working.	running, jumping rope, swimming	
Strength building: This kind of exercise builds strong muscles.	climbing stairs, hiking, throwing a baseball	
Flexibility: This kind of exercise helps your muscles and joints move easily.	ballet, karate, stretching	

What is a healthy lifestyle?

Being healthy involves many different aspects of your life. You need to eat the right foods, get enough sleep, and involve yourself in different types of exercise. That can be a lot to think about and keep track of!

But it's not that hard to do if you establish healthy habits. A habit is something you do so often that it becomes a regular part of your life. You can have healthy habits and unhealthy habits. Eating sugary snack foods every day is an unhealthy habit. Snacking on fruits and vegetables every day is a healthy habit. The nice thing is that you can control the habits you have. You can identify unhealthy habits and make changes to become more healthy. Establishing healthy habits as soon as possible in your life will help keep your body working the way it was designed to work.

Exercise is a healthy habit.▶

Here are some tips for establishing healthy habits. See if you can add more of your own ideas to the list!

Eat a variety of foods. (Try to include more whole grains and fruits and vegetables.)

Drink plenty of water.

Get between 10 and 11 hours of sleep every night.

Exercise your heart, build strong muscles, and improve your flexibility.

Have fun! Have you ever heard that laughter is the best medicine? Laughing and doing activities that you enjoy actually improve your health and help you enjoy life more.

What can you do?

First, look at your lifestyle. What are some healthy habits you have? _____

_____

_____

Give yourself a big pat on the back for the good things you are doing for your body!

Now, list your unhealthy habits. _____

_____

_____

What can you do to change those? _____

_____

_____

Health Review

All living things have a life cycle. Number the pictures in order from youngest to oldest.

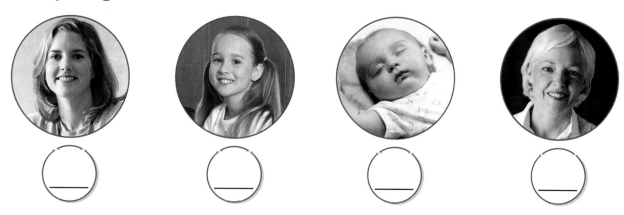

Fill in the circle next to the correct answer.

1. People need food, water, ___, and exercise to stay healthy.
   ○ candy   ○ sleep   ○ cars

2. It is important to eat a lot of ___ kinds of foods.
   ○ the same   ○ different

3. Examples of foods that are good sources of carbohydrates are pastas and ___.
   ○ chicken   ○ fish   ○ bread

4. Examples of foods that are good sources of fats are dairy products and ___.
   ○ cereal   ○ eggs   ○ apples

5. Examples of foods that are good sources of proteins are beef and ___.
   ○ celery   ○ beans   ○ pasta

6. Water is important because it helps keep your joints moving ___.
   ○ smoothly   ○ squeakily   ○ poorly

Draw a line from the food to the vitamin or mineral it contains in high amounts. Then draw a line from the vitamin or mineral to its function.

vitamin C   calcium   vitamin A   potassium

helps build   helps eyesight   helps muscles   helps wounds
strong bones   and nervous   heal
                                    system

Answer the following questions.

MyPyramid.gov
STEPS TO A HEALTHIER YOU

1. The person walking up the stairs on the left side of the pyramid represents physical activity. How many minutes of physical activity should you do most days?

_____ minutes

2. You should eat about 1½ cups of fruit each day. Should you eat more whole fruits or fruit juices? _____

3. You should eat about 3 cups of foods from the Milk group. What is another food that belongs in this group?

_____

4. You should eat between 5 and 6 ounces of grains a day. Is it more important to eat whole grains or refined grains?

_____

Match the words in column B with the descriptions in column A.

A

1. _____ This is a good cardiovascular exercise.

2. _____ Eating fruits and vegetables

3. _____ Eating too many sweets

4. _____ If you don't get enough sleep, you may have trouble doing this in school.

5. _____ This exercise builds your arm muscles.

6. _____ This exercise improves your flexibility.

B

A. stretching

B. push-ups

C. unhealthy habit

D. healthy habit

E. running

F. concentrating

List two personal health goals. (How do you plan on living a more healthy life?)

1. _____

_____

2. _____

_____

_____

_____

Vocabulary Review

Use the Word Bank to complete the sentences.

1. Non-living natural substances found in the earth are called _____. In foods, they help keep the body healthy and working properly.

2. This nutrient, called _____, provides the body with a concentrated source of energy. Examples include eggs, dairy products, meats, avocados, some nuts, and oils.

3. Substances in food that keep the body working properly are called _____. The body needs water, carbohydrates, proteins, fats, vitamins, and minerals.

4. A _____ is something you do so often that it becomes a regular part of your life.

5. A _____ is a person who recommends special diet plans to help people get or stay healthy.

6. This nutrient, called _____, helps build and repair body tissues. Examples include meats and whole grains.

7. The word _____ describes all the foods a person eats, whether healthy or unhealthy.

8. Substances found in foods that help keep the body healthy and working properly are called _____. Examples include A, B, C, D, E, and K.

My Booklet about Rocks and Soils

Name _____

Chapter 11 Vocabulary Words

geologist	mineral
humus	rock cycle
igneous rock	sedimentary rock
metamorphic rock	soil

What is a geologist?

A geologist is a scientist who studies the earth. Geologists can study many things that have to do with the earth. For example, they can study oceans, floods, earthquakes, volcanoes, and even objects in outer space. They seek to learn about the earth as it is today and what it was like in the past.

One area in which a geologist can specialize is rocks. They study what rocks are made of and how they form. They sort rocks into different groups and give each type of rock a name.

How do geologists classify rocks? What words do they use to describe what they see?

▼How would you describe these rocks?

Geologists describe rocks according to their different properties.

Color	Every rock has a color or colors that can be seen. Is it black, brown, gray, red, or some other color?
Texture	Every rock feels a certain way. Is it rough, smooth, bumpy, or jagged?
Luster	Every rock reflects light in a certain way. Is it shiny, dull, metallic, or sparkly?
Hardness	Every rock has a different level of hardness. This can be tested by scratching it. What types of material can scratch the rock?
Shape	Every rock has a shape. Is it round, square, jagged, or some other shape?

This rock has a rough texture. ▼

Rocks are everywhere! You have probably seen them in your yard, in the street, and on the playground. Rocks can be found in rivers, streams, and the ocean. If you go hiking in the woods, you will see rocks. If you go camping in the desert, you will see rocks. Some rocks are very tiny. Other rocks are huge. Have you ever seen a large boulder or a rocky cliff?

The next time you go outside, take a closer look at all the rocks around you. How many different sizes, shapes, and colors of rocks can you find?

▲Rocks can be used to make roads and buildings. What shapes do you see?

▼The Grand Canyon, in Arizona, has layers of many different colored rocks. What colors do you see?

▲There are many rocks in and near the ocean. How would you describe the sizes of these rocks?

Be a Geologist

Geologists talk about rocks using the following words: color, texture, luster, hardness, and shape. Look at these rocks and describe them in the same way a geologist would.

Obsidian

Color _____

Texture _____

Luster _____

Hardness _____

Shape _____

Talc

Color _____

Texture _____

Luster _____

Hardness _____

Shape _____

Granite

Color _____

Texture _____

Luster _____

Hardness _____

Shape _____

What are rocks made of?

Are rocks just hard pieces of dirt, or are they made of something else? If you said, "something else," you are right! Rocks are made of minerals. A mineral is a non-living, natural substance found in the earth.

Some rocks are made of more than one mineral. Granite is a good example of this. It is made of quartz, feldspar, and mica. Other rocks, like gold, silver, and limestone, are made of only one mineral.

You probably know more minerals than you realize. Look around your classroom. Do you see any chalk? Chalk is made from a mineral called limestone. Do you have a pencil on your desk? The "lead" in your pencil is made from a mineral called graphite. Most gemstones are minerals. Diamonds, rubies, emeralds, and sapphires are all minerals. People use these minerals to make jewelry because they are so beautiful. Can you think of any other minerals?

▲Limestone stalactites are found in caves.

Pyrite is called fool's gold ▶ because its appearance might trick you into thinking you have discovered a gold nugget!

▼Emeralds are valuable gemstones that come from the mineral beryl.

After an emerald has been cut and polished, it looks like this.▶

Looking at Minerals

Geologists describe minerals in the same ways that they describe rocks. They look at the color, texture, luster, hardness, and shapes of minerals. How would you describe these minerals?

Sulfur

Color _____

Texture _____

Luster _____

Hardness _____

Shape _____

Parrot Wing
Copper Ore

Color _____

Texture _____

Luster _____

Hardness _____

Shape _____

Smoky
Quartz and
Amazonite

Color _____

Texture _____

Luster _____

Hardness _____

Shape _____

How are rocks formed?

Some rocks are formed when small pieces of minerals pile up in layers. These are called sedimentary rocks. Wind or water breaks off little pieces of earth and they settle at the bottom of rivers, lakes, and oceans. Pressure causes these pieces of earth to stick together, harden, and form rocks. Some examples of sedimentary rocks are sandstone, limestone, and shale.

Sandstone

Other rocks are formed when magma, melted rock under the earth, cools and hardens. These are called igneous rocks. Sometimes volcanoes erupt and shoot out lava. Magma that is above the earth's surface is called lava. When the lava cools and hardens it also forms igneous rocks. Some examples of igneous rocks are granite, basalt, and obsidian.

Granite

Arches National Park in Utah is filled with sandstone formations.

Some rocks are formed when heat and pressure are applied to igneous and sedimentary rocks. The heat and pressure cause these rocks to change or "morph" into another kind of rock. These are called metamorphic rocks. Examples of metamorphic rocks are marble, slate, and gneiss.

Marble

Marble can be carved ▶
into statues like this one.

What kind of rock?

Draw a line from the rock to how it was formed.

metamorphic

igneous

sedimentary

This rock was made when lava cooled and hardened.

This rock was made when layers of minerals built up at the bottom of a lake.

This rock was made when heat and pressure changed an igneous rock into another rock.

Do rocks change their form?

You have learned how sedimentary, igneous, and metamorphic rocks are formed. But did you know that these rocks don't always stay the same? All three forms of rock can be changed into the other two forms. This is done through a process called the **rock cycle**.

Sedimentary

Sedimentary rocks can melt, cool, and harden to form igneous rocks.

Wind and water can wear down igneous rocks and form sedimentary rocks.

Igneous

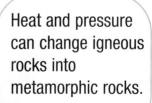

Heat and pressure can change sedimentary rocks into metamorphic rocks.

Metamorphic rocks can melt, cool, and harden to form igneous rocks.

Heat and pressure can change igneous rocks into metamorphic rocks.

Wind and water can wear down metamorphic rocks and form sedimentary rocks.

Metamorphic

How is the rock cycle at work today?

The earth is always changing. Wind and water erode mountains and form sedimentary rocks. Volcanoes erupt and form igneous rocks. Heat and pressure under the earth's surface form metamorphic rocks.

Look at the picture and use the Word Bank to identify where each type of rock is being formed.

Word Bank		
Sedimentary	Igneous	Metamorphic

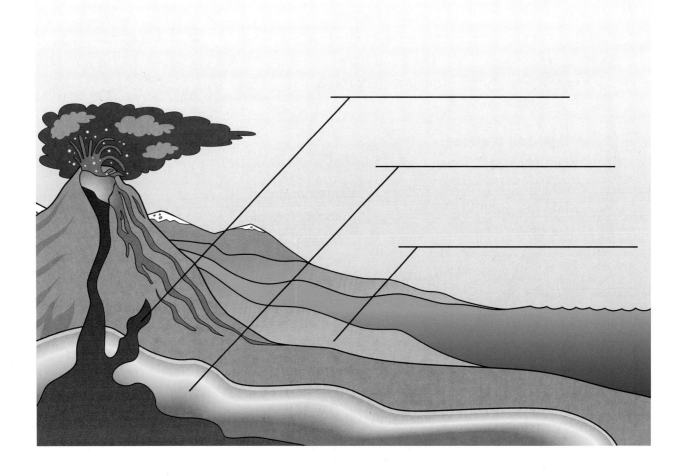

What is soil?

You might think that soil is only made of tiny pieces of rocks, but it is actually made of a lot more. Soil is the loose material that covers the surface of the earth. It supports plant growth and is made of both living and non-living things.

Soil is made of four main things. First, it contains tiny pieces of rocks and minerals. It also contains humus, the decaying plant and animal matter that helps plants grow. Between the tiny rocks and humus are spaces called pores. These pores hold water and air. They also provide passageways for earthworms, ants, and other small animals that live in the soil. So soil is made of rocks and minerals, humus, water, and air.

clay

potting soil

sand

Soil is important because plants need it to grow. Plants are our main food source, so it is important that we take care of the soil. Soil is always being made, but it takes a long time to make and

it is easily damaged. Wind and water can blow soil away, farming can remove all the nutrients, and heavy machinery can compact the soil. Scientists and farmers are working to come up with new ways to conserve soil.

What is soil made of?

Draw and label the four things that make up soil. You may also include animals that live in the soil.

How are rocks, minerals, and soils used?

One of the reasons God created rocks, minerals, and soils is so that people could use them. In fact, people have been using rocks, minerals, and soils for a long time!  You probably know that buildings can be made out of stone, beautiful jewelry is made from minerals like gold or silver, and soil is used to grow plants. But perhaps you aren't familiar with these other uses for rocks, minerals, and soils.

Look out your classroom window. The glass window you are looking through is made of quartz. Is there a sidewalk around your school? Sidewalks are made with cement, which is a mixture of sand, crushed gravel, and ground limestone. You might also be surprised to learn that computers and video games use silicon chips, which are made from the mineral quartz.

Have you ever seen a china tea set? China is made from clay. The plates you eat dinner on

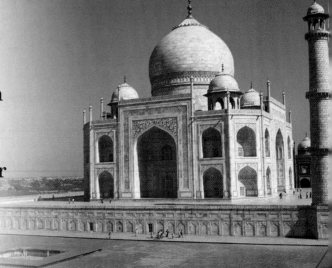

every night were probably made from clay. People also use rocks to make statues and monuments. Many great artists have used rocks to create their art. Can you think of any other uses for rocks, minerals, and soils?

How are They Used?

Look at the pictures and write about how rocks, minerals, or soils are being used.

1.
_____
_____
_____
_____

2.
_____
_____
_____

3.
_____
_____
_____
_____

4.
_____
_____
_____

5.
_____
_____
_____

How do we study rocks and minerals?

Geologists describe rocks and minerals according to their color, texture, luster, hardness, and shape. Describe these rocks and minerals as a geologist would.

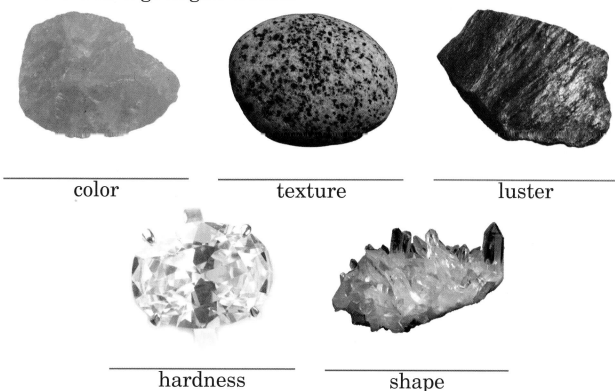

color   texture   luster

hardness   shape

Sedimentary, Igneous, or Metamorphic?

Read about how each rock is formed. Circle the correct name of each rock type.

1. Granite is formed when magma or lava cools and hardens.
   a. sedimentary   b. igneous   c. metamorphic

2. Marble is formed when heat and pressure are applied to a sedimentary rock.
   a. sedimentary   b. igneous   c. metamorphic

3. Sandstone is formed when layers of minerals pile up, stick to each other, and harden.
   a. sedimentary   b. igneous   c. metamorphic

How do rocks change form?

Write the letters in the blanks to show how rocks can change from one form to another through the rock cycle.

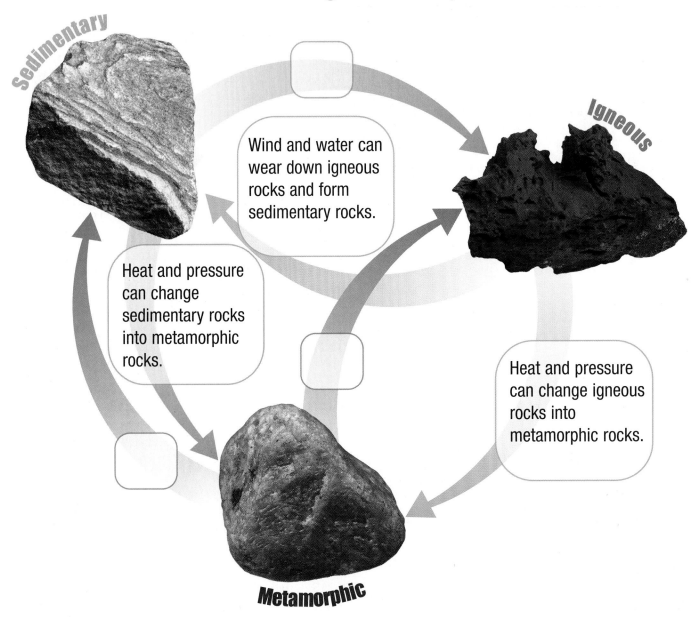

A. Sedimentary rocks can melt, cool, and harden to form igneous rocks.

B. Metamorphic rocks can melt, cool, and harden to form igneous rocks.

C. Wind and water can wear down metamorphic rocks and form sedimentary rocks.

What is soil?

List the things that make up soil.

_____

_____

_____

_____

How do we use rocks, minerals, and soils?

Read about each picture. Write another way that people use rocks, minerals, or soils.

This building was made with rocks. What is another way people can use rocks?

_____

_____

This window was made from the mineral quartz. What is another way people can use minerals?

_____

_____

This dish was made from clay. What is another way people can use soil?

_____

_____

Vocabulary Review

Use the Word Bank to complete the sentences.

1. Rock that forms when magma or lava cools and hardens is called _____ rock.

2. A scientist who studies the earth is called a _____.

3. The decaying plant and animal matter in soil that helps plants grow is called _____.

4. Rock that forms when heat and pressure are applied to igneous or sedimentary rocks is called _____ rock.

5. Rock that forms when layers of minerals pile up, stick to each other, and harden is called _____ rock.

6. The loose material that covers the surface of the earth and supports plant growth is called _____.

7. Non-living, natural substances found in the earth are called _____.

8. The process through which rocks change from one form to another is called the rock _____.

Word Bank		
geologist	minerals	sedimentary
igneous	metamorphic	cycle
soil	humus	

My Booklet about the Earth's Surface

Name _____

canyon	lake
coastline	landform
continent	mountain
elevation	plain
erosion	river
geographer	valley

How do you describe the earth?

If you look at the earth from outer space, you can see that most of our planet's surface is covered in water. In fact, almost 70 percent of the earth is covered in water. That's a lot of water! But what about the parts that aren't covered in water? What do they look like?

The earth's land is divided into seven major land masses called continents. These continents have a variety of different landforms. Landforms are features of the earth's surface. There are mountains, plains, valleys, canyons, and coasts. There are also a variety of water features present on the earth's surface. Examples of water features are lakes and rivers.

Photo courtesy of NASA.

▲ This is a nighttime photograph taken from space. You can see lights on every continent but one. Which one has no lights? Why is this so?

People who live in cold, snowy places sometimes use sleds for traveling. ▼

Some kinds of plants and animals live only in specific areas. Mountain goats only live on mountains. Cacti grow mainly in the desert. But God designed people to live all over the planet. They live on high mountains and they also live in low valleys. Some people live near lakes and rivers and some live in deserts where there isn't very much water. People can survive in most of the earth's different environments.

People in Egypt have built great civilizations in the desert.

▲Mountain goats live on high mountains.

People in Asia use yaks to plow their fields. ▶

Geographers are scientists who study the earth's surface. Making maps, studying how landforms change, and observing how people interact with the land are just some of the things they do. They recognize that the environment affects how people live.

For example, people who live near mountains have to deal with very cold temperatures. To survive, they need warm houses and clothing. People who live in warmer areas don't need to wear as much clothing to survive. People who live near lakes, rivers, and oceans may use boats for transportation. People who don't live near water have no need for boats. How does your environment affect you?

◀People who live near the ocean use boats for fishing.

What is it like where you live?

Circle the words and phrases that describe where you live.

- **Land:**

  mountains   valleys   canyons   plains   hills

- **Water:**

  ocean   lake   river   stream   pond

- **Temperatures:**

  mostly hot temperatures   both hot and cold temperatures

  mostly cold temperatures

- **Rainfall:**

  a lot of rain   some rain   not very much rain   no rain

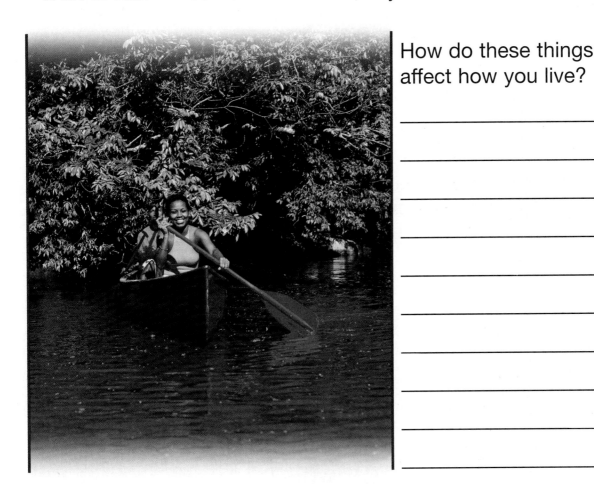

How do these things affect how you live?

_____

_____

_____

_____

_____

_____

_____

_____

_____

What are mountains?

Mountains are landforms that usually rise at least 2,000 feet (610 m) above the earth's surface. Generally, mountains are found in groups called ranges. When people talk about the height of a mountain they usually refer to its elevation. This refers to how high land rises above sea level. The highest mountain in the world is Mt. Everest. It has an elevation of 29,028 feet (8,848 m) above sea level.

Because mountains are so high, they affect the weather significantly. As wind blows against mountains, it rises and cools. Water vapor in the air condenses and forms clouds, which then forms precipitation. The side of the mountain that the wind blows up usually gets more rain and snow than the other side.

Yaks are native to Tibet.▶

Tibet, located in the Himalayan Mountains, is the highest region on earth. Because of this, it is sometimes called the "Roof of the World."

The higher you go up on a mountain, the colder it gets and the less oxygen there is to breathe. For this reason, people and wildlife live at different heights on a mountain. People usually don't live higher than 10,000 feet above sea level because it is too

cold, rugged, and there is not enough oxygen in the air. An exception to this is the city of La Paz, Bolivia. It is located in the Andes Mountains and is over 12,000 feet above sea level.

◀A llama looks over the ancient ruins of Machu Picchu. The Incas built this city high in the Andes Mountains.

How are mountains useful to people?

Mountains are useful to people because they are often sources of valuable natural resources such as minerals, timber, and water. Some mountain slopes are especially good for growing crops. Look at the pictures and describe how people are using the mountain.

What is a valley?

A valley is an area of low-lying land that is surrounded by higher ground. Valleys usually have a stream or a river running through them. The streams and rivers begin at higher ground and flow to the lower ground, ultimately ending at a lake or an ocean.

One of the longest and broadest valleys in the world is the Mississippi River Valley. It stretches across the United States from the North to the South. The Mississippi River flows down the center of this valley. The deepest valley in the world is the Indus River Valley in Kashmir. One of the earliest human civilizations flourished in this valley because of its fertile soil and plentiful water supply.

Some valleys are useful to people because they have fertile soil for growing crops. ▼

Valleys, like other landforms, are constantly changing. Rain, wind, and moving water in rivers and streams are always loosening material on the valley walls. This material eventually falls into the running water and is carried downstream. The removal of rock and soil by wind and water is called erosion.

A canyon is a valley that is very deep and has steep, rocky cliffs on its sides. Canyons can begin with a crack in the earth's crust caused by an earthquake. Rivers run through canyons and continually wear away the rock, making them deeper and deeper as the years go by. One of the most famous and spectacular canyons in the world is the Grand Canyon in Arizona.

How do valleys change?

Look at the picture. Describe how rain, wind, and moving water could change the shape of this canyon.

_____

_____

_____

_____

_____

_____

Why live on a plain?

Plains are mostly flat, level areas of land that cover about one-third of the earth's land surface. Plains are found on all continents except Antarctica. Some plains are deserts. There is very little plant life in these areas. However, other plains have a lot of plant life.

Plains have become the major areas of human populations for many reasons. Grassy plains usually have nutrient-rich soil that is well-suited for growing crops. Plains are also used as pastures for grazing animals such as cattle and sheep. The flat surface of the land makes it easier for people to farm, build roads, and navigate rivers. Because flat surfaces are easier to travel across, people can travel easily from one city to another across a plain.

Most of the pioneers' journey was across the Great Plains.

▲ Citys are often built on plains.

▲ The Serengeti Plain, in Africa, is home to many animals.

▲ Some plains are deserts.

Mesopotamia

Mesopotamia is a plain located between the Tigris and Euphrates rivers. Found in modern-day Iraq, it is the site of one of the world's earliest civilizations.

Many of the events in the Old Testament take place in Mesopotamia. Have you ever heard of Babylon or Nineveh? Both of these cities were located in ancient Mesopotamia. Throughout ancient history, rulers fought to gain control of this fertile plain.

Look at the map and identify the modern countries that are located in Mesopotamia.

Word Bank
Iran
Iraq
Turkey
Saudi Arabia
Jordan
Kuwait

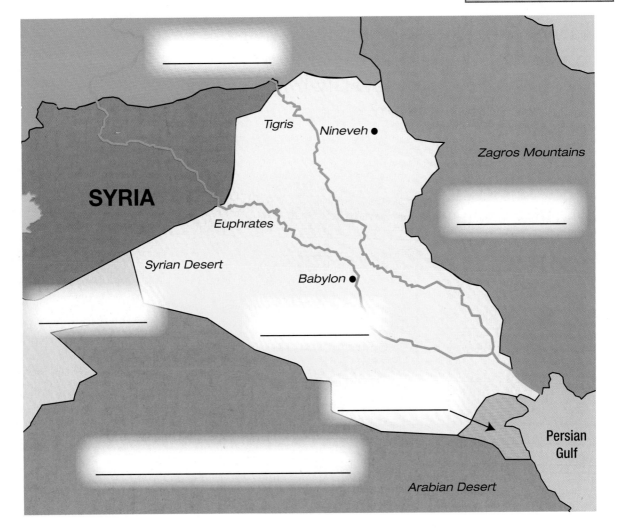

Why are lakes and rivers important?

You would probably agree that water is important and necessary to your life, but do you know where it comes from? Where do we get the water we need for bathing and drinking?

Much of our water comes from lakes and rivers. Lakes are large bodies of water surrounded by land. Many communities depend heavily on the water supply from large lakes such as Lake Superior in North America or Lake Baikal in Asia.

A river is a body of freshwater that flows from an upland source to a large lake or to the sea. The earliest human civilizations began near rivers. This is because rivers provide a water supply, a food supply, a means of transportation, and protection from enemies.

▲ The city of Chicago is located on the southwestern shore of Lake Michigan.

People use rivers for transportation and recreation. ▶

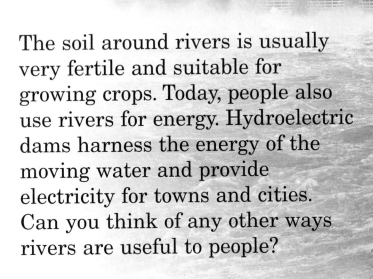

The soil around rivers is usually very fertile and suitable for growing crops. Today, people also use rivers for energy. Hydroelectric dams harness the energy of the moving water and provide electricity for towns and cities. Can you think of any other ways rivers are useful to people?

Name the River

Many of the great cities of the world have been built beside rivers. Each of these cities is located near a river. Look at a map and write the name of the continent and river that goes with each city.

Continent	City	River
1. _____	Cairo	_____
2. _____	Baghdad	_____
3. _____	Paris	_____
4. _____	Washington, D.C.	_____
5. _____	London	_____

Do coastlines stay the same?

Have you ever spent time on a beach? Beaches are a part of the coastline, which is the place where the land meets the ocean. Since all land masses have edges that touch the ocean, there are a lot of coastlines around the world. Although every continent has coastlines, they don't all look the same. Some are rocky, some are sandy, some have high towering cliffs, and others are very flat.

Coastlines do not always stay the same shape. Erosion by water and wind can gradually change the shape of a coastline. For example, the constant pounding of waves against a rocky cliff gradually wears down the rocks. This forms caves and arches. On sandy beaches, waves roll sand up a beach and then drag it back down. This constant movement causes slight changes in the coastline's shape. Wind also affects the shape of a coastline by removing sand from one area and depositing it in another.

Coastlines are important to people for several reasons. Ships anchor in harbors and are loaded and unloaded at ports. This is one of the main ways goods are transported from one country to another. People also have large fishing industries on coastlines because the ocean is an important food source for people. Coastlines are also popular vacation areas. Tourism is one of the major businesses of many of the world's beautiful beaches.

Sandy Beaches

Sand is made of tiny pieces of minerals, rocks, and shells. The color of sand gives a clue about what it is made of. Most sand is made of the mineral quartz and is yellow in color, but there are some other colors that might surprise you. Color the sand to match the description.

The black sand beaches of Hawaii and Tahiti were formed from volcanic lava.

The Bermuda islands have beaches of pale pink sand. The sand was made from pieces of red shell.

The white sandy beaches of Barbados were formed by tiny pieces of white shell.

Earth's Surface Review

The earth's surface has many different features. What does it look like where you live? Are there tall mountains or flat plains? Do you live near a lake or a river? Where you live affects how you live. Look at these pictures and identify the name of the landform or water feature.

A. mountain   E. lake
B. valley   F. river
C. canyon   G. coastline
D. plain

Mountains can affect the weather. Draw arrows to show how mountains push wind up. Inside the cloud, write how precipitation forms.

_____

_____

_____

_____

The earth's surface is always changing. Describe how erosion by water and wind could change the shape of this canyon.

_____

_____

_____

Describe how water and wind could change the shape of this coastline.

_____

_____

_____

How are these landforms and water features useful to people?

1. ____ Mountains

2. ____ Valleys

3. ____ Plains

4. ____ Lakes and rivers

5. ____ Coastlines

A. These are well-suited for growing crops because they have good soil and are very flat.

B. These are important sources of fresh water.

C. These are used for their harbors.

D. These are often sources of valuable natural resources such as minerals, timber, and water.

E. These often have good soil and a plentiful water supply.

Where you live affects how you live. Describe how each of the following things affects you personally.

• Landforms: _____

_____

• Water features: _____

_____

• Temperatures: _____

_____

• Weather: _____

_____

Vocabulary Review

Use the Word Bank to complete the sentences.

1. A _____ is a mostly flat, level area of land.

2. The place where the land meets the ocean is the _____.

3. One of the earth's seven major land masses is called a _____.

4. An area of low-lying land that is surrounded by higher ground is called a _____.

5. A scientist who studies the earth's surface is called a _____.

6. A feature of the earth's surface is called a _____.

7. How high a mountain rises above sea level is called _____.

8. A large body of water surrounded by land is called a _____.

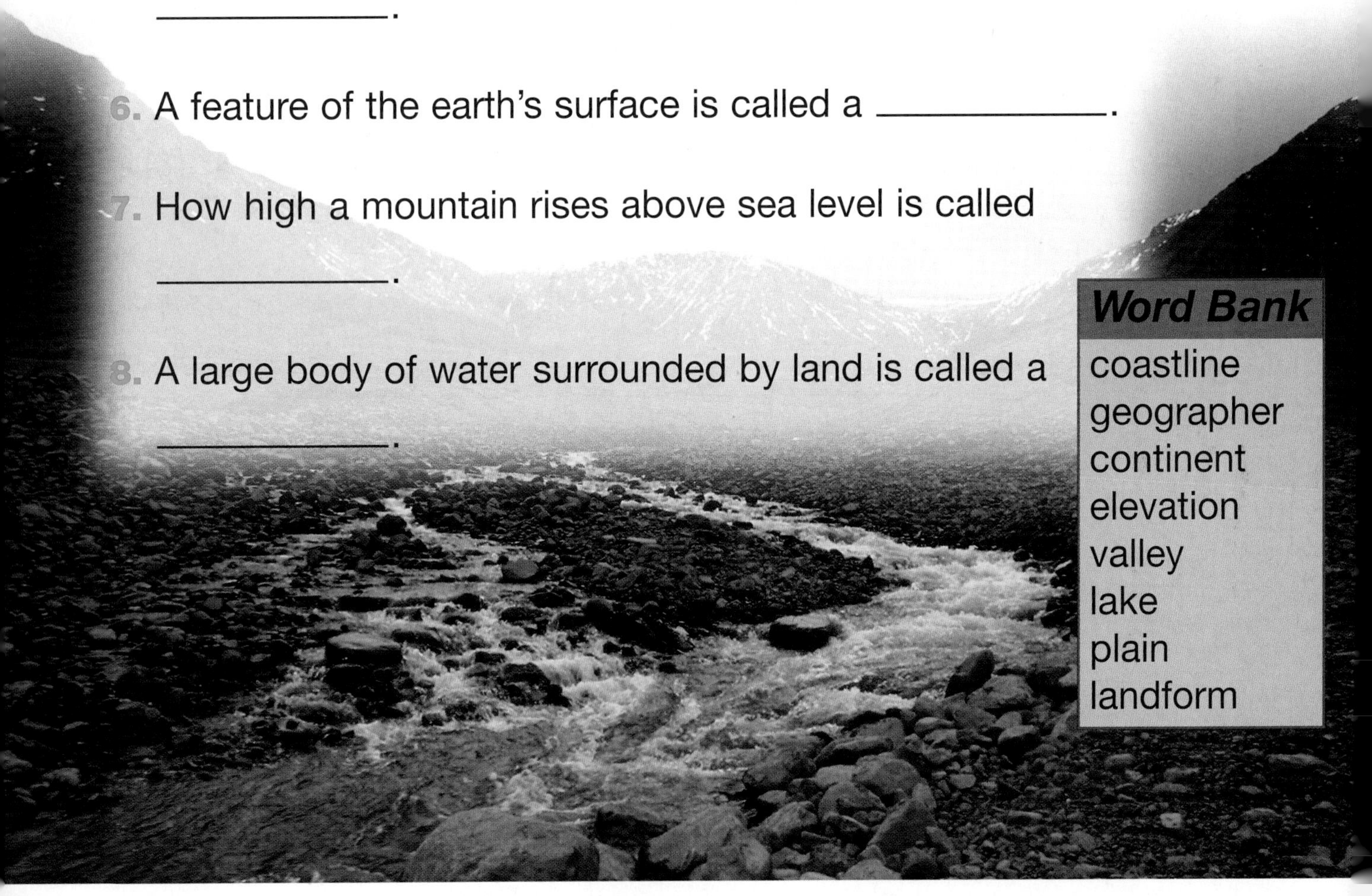

Word Bank

coastline
geographer
continent
elevation
valley
lake
plain
landform

My Booklet about Changes in the Earth's Surface

Name _____

active volcano	fault
avalanche	landform
cartographer	landslide
dormant volcano	mudslide
earthquake	tsunami
erosion	volcano

What can cause landform changes?

Do you ever wonder if the earth looks the same as it did before you were born? Do landforms change or stay the same?

A landform is a feature of the earth's surface. Mountains, valleys, rivers, and canyons are all types of landforms. These landforms constantly change due to wind, water, ice, and forces under the earth's surface.

Wind can change landforms. When it blows, it moves particles of rock and soil from one place to another. As the wind blows, these tiny particles hit larger rocks, and loosen more particles that can be carried away. These particles are then deposited elsewhere on earth.

Wind can blow sand quickly enough to cover entire landforms.

Landforms can be changed by water. Every time it rains, water splashes to the ground and loosens particles of soil. Water flowing across the earth's surface moves these particles to another location. The removal of rock and soil by wind and water is called erosion.

Ice can cause change to landforms. When water fills the cracks in rocks and then freezes, it expands. This causes small particles and large chunks of rocks to break off. The small particles can then be carried away by the wind or moving water. Glaciers, or large masses of ice, can wear away land as it melts. The combination of pressure and scraping from the glacier will eventually wear away the land underneath the glacier.

Rivers and streams carry loosened rock and soil downstream where it is deposited onto plains, and into oceans, lakes, and other rivers.

There are also forces within the earth that can cause landforms to change suddenly. Volcanoes and earthquakes are caused by movements under the surface of the earth.

Since landforms are constantly changing, the maps we use must be updated to show these changes. People who make maps are called cartographers. They work closely with scientists and geologists to record the various changes in landforms. Using aerial photography, satellite images, and other measurement devices, they design many different types of maps. One type of map they make is called a relief map. It shows where all the mountains, valleys, and rivers are located in a particular area. Why would a relief map need to be updated?

Hot lava flows into the ocean producing steam and adding to the land.

Identifying changes

Photo A was taken over 100 years ago. Photo B is a recent photo of the same area.

Photo A

Photo B

Study the two photos. What things have changed over time?

_____

_____

_____

What could have caused these changes?

_____

_____

_____

How can landforms change suddenly?

Erosion can change landforms gradually, but did you know that it can also change them suddenly?

When too much rainwater or melting snow sinks into the side of a mountain, rocks and soil are loosened. If the mountainside is weakened enough, gravity will cause a landslide to occur. A landslide is a large amount of dry soil and rock that slides down a steep slope. A large landslide can cause major changes to nearby landforms. Large boulders tumbling down mountainsides can fill canyons below. They can also block the flow of rivers and cause flooding.

Avalanches are similar to landslides. An avalanche is a large amount of snow that slides down the side of a mountain. When a large mass of snow slides down the side of a mountain, it can carry large amounts of rock, soil, and trees with it.

Erosion can also occur in areas where wildfires have burned away all the plants and trees that anchor the soil. Without plants' roots holding the soil in place, water can quickly soak and loosen an area such as a mountainside. A mudslide occurs when a large amount of wet soil and rock slides down a steep slope. These mudslides can become so powerful that they wash away homes and reshape mountains.

Understanding Rapid Erosion

Write answers to the following questions.

1. What is the difference between a landslide and a mudslide?

_____

_____

_____

2. How can an avalanche change a landform?

_____

_____

_____

_____

What changes do volcanoes cause?

A volcano is an opening in the earth's crust that spews out lava, hot ash, and gases during an eruption. Some volcanoes leak material slowly. Other volcanoes have violent eruptions in which the lava, ash, and gases are blown out.

An active volcano is one that continues to erupt. A dormant volcano is one that has not erupted in recent years.

Mount Fuji is a dormant volcano. ▶
It last erupted in 1708.

Mount St. Helens is an active volcano.

Volcanoes can cause sudden changes to landforms by forming new landmasses. For example, Surtsey Island in Iceland is being formed by a volcano. It began forming in 1963 and is still increasing in size.

Volcanoes can also destroy landforms and water features. The lava and hot ash that are ejected from a volcano can bury a lake or block the flow of a river. The area surrounding a volcano can be drastically changed by a volcanic eruption.

The Hawaiian islands were formed by volcanic activity.

Because of this lava flow, road maps in Hawaii will have to be changed.

Discovering Volcanoes

1. What is the difference between an active and a dormant volcano?

_____

_____

2. Explain how an erupting volcano could change landforms.

_____

_____

What makes the earth move?

Scientists believe that the earth's crust consists of thick plates that float on top of the liquid mantle. These plates are constantly moving, which can cause them to push on or collide with one another. Sometimes this movement can cause an earthquake.

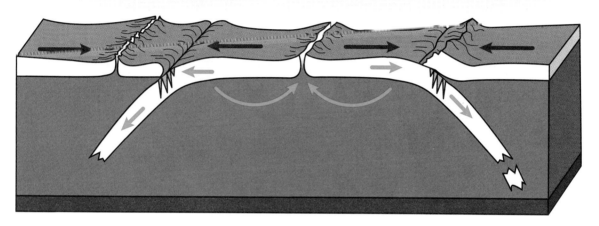

An earthquake is the shaking of the earth's surface that is caused by the sudden movement of the earth's crust. Earthquakes usually occur along a fault, which is a crack in the earth's crust.

Most faults cannot be seen. An exception is the San Andreas Fault in California. Because of this fault and others, California has over 1,000 earthquakes a year. Most are too small to be felt by humans.

Photo courtesy of Chris Walls, Earth Consultants International

An earthquake can cause the ground to split apart leaving large cracks. ▲

Effects of an Earthquake

Use the photo of the landscape to answer the following questions.

1. How might an earthquake change the river?

_____

_____

2. How might an earthquake change the hills?

_____

_____

_____

What is a tsunami?

You know that volcanoes and earthquakes occur on land, but did you know that they can also occur deep underwater on the ocean floor?

These underwater volcanic eruptions and earthquakes can cause a series of large ocean waves called a tsunami. In the deep ocean, these waves are only about $3\frac{1}{2}$ feet (1 m) high but as they move to shallower, coastal waters, the waves grow. Some tsunami waves have reached 100 feet (30 m) tall. That's as tall as a 12-story building! These waves can also travel at speeds of up to 500 miles (805 km) per hour.

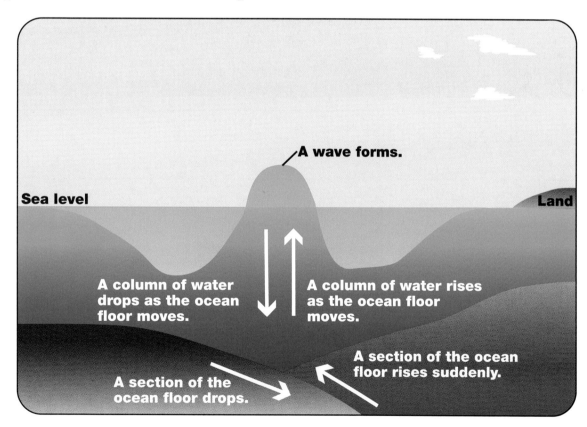

A wave forms.

Sea level

Land

A column of water drops as the ocean floor moves.

A column of water rises as the ocean floor moves.

A section of the ocean floor rises suddenly.

A section of the ocean floor drops.

The power, speed, and volume of water in a tsunami can cause serious damage to coastlines. The water can carry debris, soil, and sand inland for miles. The powerful waves can destroy entire islands.

Understanding Tsunamis

Examine the landform before a tsunami. Draw a picture of what the area might look like after a tsunami.

How do scientists study volcanoes and earthquakes?

Scientists have many tools to help them study the changes in the earth's surface. Many different types of scientists use these tools to learn about the earth.

There are sensors installed on active volcanoes that relay information about gases and chemical changes within a volcano. Satellite-based systems monitor the physical changes of the volcano's surface. Scientists use this information to help them learn more about processes inside the earth.

Scientists use a seismograph to measure vibrations, called seismic waves, caused by moving plates in the earth's crust. Seismographs help scientists learn more about the earth's interior.

Seismic-monitoring stations and sea-level gauges monitor seismic activity on the ocean's floor. The Pacific Tsunami Warning Centers located in Hawaii and Alaska use equipment to detect earthquakes and changes in the ocean level. This information can help determine when tsunamis are likely to occur.

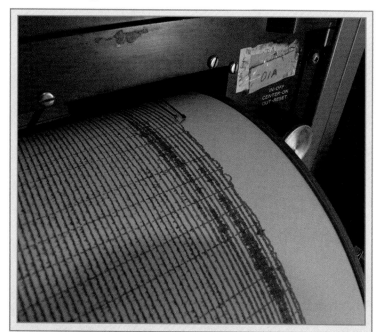

◄On a seismograph, a needle records seismic activity on a rotating drum.

Photo courtesy of Tom Pfeiffer/www.decadevolcano.net.

Two members of the Alaska Volcano Observatory work on a seismometer which is located south of Mount Spurr in Alaska. ▶

Photo courtesy of Sigrun Hreinsdottir, Alaska Volcano Observatory.

Monitoring Change

Write the letters of the tools that scientists use to monitor earthquakes, tsunamis, and volcanoes. Some choices may be used more than once.

Earthquake	Tsunami	Volcano
_____	_____	_____
_____	_____	_____

A. a machine that measures vibrations

B. a machine that monitors gases

C. a machine that monitors sea level

D. a satellite that monitors surface changes

Changes in the Earth's Surface Review

The earth's surface is constantly changing. These changes can be gradual or sudden. Wind, water, and ice can cause slow changes, while landslides, avalanches, volcanoes, earthquakes, and tsunamis can cause sudden changes.

Fill in the circle next to the word that completes the sentence.

1. A landform is a feature of the earth's _____.
   ○ interior   ○ atmosphere   ○ surface

2. Erosion is the removal of rocks and soil by _____ and wind.
   ○ water   ○ sun   ○ trees

3. A _____ is a person who makes maps.
   ○ oceanographer   ○ cartographer   ○ biographer

This volcanic eruption has changed the area around the mountain.

How do these earth-changing events affect the earth's surface?
Draw a line from the word in column A to the sentences in
column B.

A

1. volcano

2. earthquake

3. avalanche

4. tsunami

5. mudslide

B

A. Large amounts of snow sliding down a mountain can destroy trees, fill canyons, and block the flow of rivers.

B. Wet soil and rock falling down a steep slope can wash away trees and plants in its path. Mud and rocks can fill rivers and canyons below.

C. Islands and mountains can be formed or destroyed when lava and hot ash are spewed out onto the land. Lakes can be buried and rivers can change course as lava fills these areas.

D. Movement of the earth's plates can cause large boulders to fill up valleys and canyons. Rivers can change their courses and lakes can drain as a result of cracks in the earth's surface.

E. Large waves can wash coastlines away along with the rocks and soil nearby. Trees can be uprooted and debris can be carried inland for miles.

Volcanoes, earthquakes, and tsunamis can cause many changes to the earth's surface. Scientists monitor these changes to learn more about the earth.

Describe some of the effects that a volcano can have on a landform.

_____

_____

_____

_____

_____

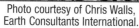
Photo courtesy of Chris Walls, Earth Consultants International.

Describe how an earthquake can change a landform.

_____

_____

_____

_____

_____

Describe how a tsunami can change a landform.

_____

_____

_____

_____

_____

Vocabulary Review

Use the Word Bank to complete the sentences.

1. A crack in the earth's crust is called a

   _____.

2. A volcano that has not erupted in recent
   years is called a _____ volcano.

3. A person who makes maps is called a

   _____.

4. A _____ is a large amount of wet soil
   and rock that slides down a steep slope.

5. A _____ is a feature of the earth's surface.

6. An _____ is the shaking of the
   earth's surface that is caused by the sudden movement of
   the earth's crust.

7. An opening in the earth's crust that spews out lava, hot
   ash, and gases during an eruption is a _____.

8. An _____ is a large amount of snow
   that slides down the side of a mountain.

9. The removal of rock or soil by water or wind is called

   _____.

10. A _____ is a series of large ocean waves
    caused by an underwater earthquake or volcanic eruption.

My Booklet about
The Solar System

Name _____

Chapter 14 Vocabulary Words

- astronaut
- axis
- moon phase
- orbit
- planet
- probe
- revolution
- rotation
- satellite
- solar system
- star
- telescope

How do scientists explore space?

Have you ever wondered what outer space is like? People have wondered for a long time. Thousands of years ago, people studied the sun, moon, planets, and stars. They used these observations to make clocks and calendars. In the 1600s people made telescopes. A telescope is an instrument that is used to observe faraway objects by making them appear larger and closer. Scientists improved the original telescope and then discovered a way to send telescopes into space. Space telescopes are equipped with computers and cameras to collect data and transmit it back to scientists on earth.

NASA launched the Spitzer Space Telescope in August of 2003. The telescope is able to look deep into space and will help scientists learn more about the universe.▼

Illustration courtesy of NASA/JPL-Caltech

Scientists also send space probes and satellites into space. A **probe** is an unmanned spacecraft that is sent into space to collect information. Space probes can travel to places that are too dangerous for humans. Computers and radio signals guide the probes as they travel through space.

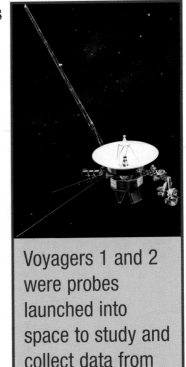

Voyagers 1 and 2 were probes launched into space to study and collect data from the outer planets.

Photo courtesy of NASA

▲ This photo of Saturn was taken by the Voyager 2 probe.

Another way scientists study space is with satellites. A **satellite** is an object that revolves around a larger object in space. Satellites are sent into space to transmit television and radio signals from one part of the world to another. They can also take photos of the object they are circling.

Scientists soon discovered how to send people into space. Manned space shuttles now carry astronauts and equipment. An astronaut is a person who is trained to travel into space. Astronauts conduct experiments studying the effects of space travel on plants, animals, and even themselves. Some shuttle missions allow the astronauts to collect rock and dust particles. Some astronauts are sent to repair equipment already in space. Other missions include launching satellites, probes, and telescopes from

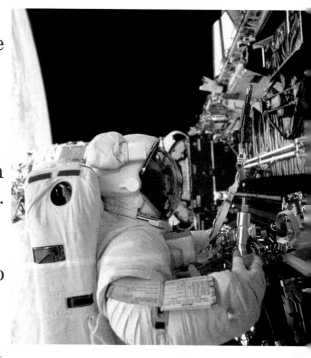

the shuttle itself. Sometimes, shuttle missions are used to pick up astronauts living at the International Space Station and bring them back to earth.

Scientists now use all three ways to study space: telescopes, unmanned probes and satellites, and astronauts. They learn about other planets, examine objects in space, and study how people can live in space. Because space is so big, there will always be more to learn. Can you think of anything else that could be explored in space?

Photo courtesy of NASA

There can be two to six crew members aboard the International Space Station performing experiments and conducting research. Scientists gather this data to use in improving medical and biological technology. The ISS orbits the earth and can be viewed from time to time from earth.

Exploring Space

Draw a line from the name to how it would best be used.

1. probe   relaying radio signals back to earth

2. astronaut   making objects far away appear closer

3. telescope   exploring a very hot planet

4. satellite   observing and doing experiments in space

Name three ways scientists study objects in space.

1._____

2._____

3._____

Why do you think we should study space?_____

_____

_____

_____

What is the solar system?

Our solar system consists of the sun and all the objects that revolve around it. Nine of these objects are planets. A planet is a large body of rock or gas that revolves around the sun.

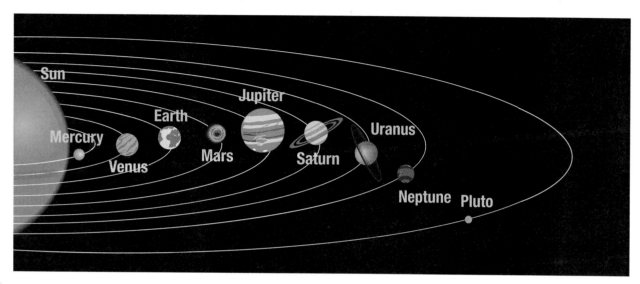

To revolve means to move around another object. When an object moves all the way around another object it has completed a revolution. It takes the earth about 365 days to make one complete revolution around the sun. The path that an object follows as it revolves around another object is called an orbit. As each planet revolves around the sun, it follows an orbit. An orbit in our solar system is elliptical, or oval.

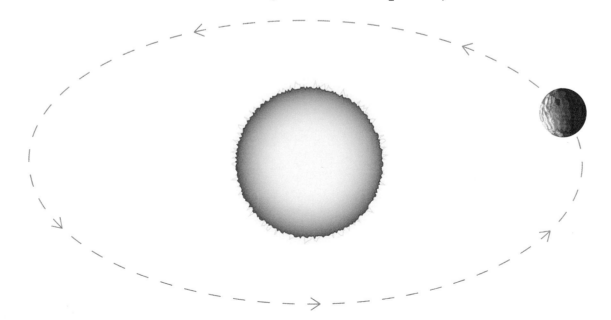

The sun is not a planet but rather a very bright star. A star is a glowing ball of burning gases. The center of the sun is extremely hot. Energy is produced by the processes that take place inside the sun. Some of this energy then travels through space and reaches the earth in about 8 minutes. The energy from the sun provides us with heat and light which are needed for life to exist on earth.

Fun Sun Fact:
Did you know that the sun is over 93 million miles (150 million km) away from earth? It would take a space probe over 7 months to reach the sun, but it would melt before it got there!

Understanding Our Solar System

Fill in the circle next to the correct answer.

1. The path a planet follows around the sun is called an _____.
   ○ object   ○ orbit

2. The sun is a _____.
   ○ star   ○ planet

3. When a planet moves all the way around the sun it has completed one _____.
   ○ revolution   ○ path

4. The _____ includes the sun and all other objects that orbit around it.
   ○ planets   ○ solar system

What are the four inner planets?

You learned that all planets revolve around the sun, but did you know that they also rotate? To rotate means to turn around a center. A rotation is the spinning of an object on its axis. An axis is an imaginary line that goes through the middle of an object. Each planet rotates on its own axis the way a wheel rotates on an axle. Earth's axis goes from the North Pole to the South Pole.

Beginning at the sun, the first four planets in order are Mercury, Venus, Earth, and Mars. These four planets are called the inner planets. They all have hard, rocky surfaces. However, each planet is unique in its size, its distance from the sun, and the time it takes to orbit the sun.

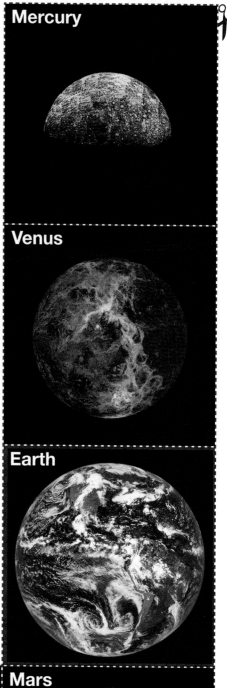

Mercury

Venus

Earth

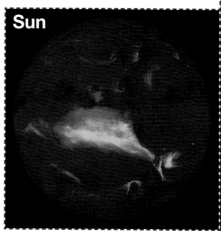

Sun

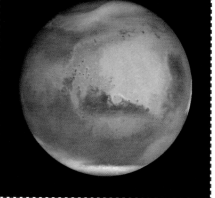

Mars

Photos courtesy of NASA.

diameter
3,000 miles

distance from sun
36 million miles

one revolution
88 Earth days

one rotation
59 Earth days

moons
0

---

diameter
7,500 miles

distance from sun
67 million miles

one revolution
225 Earth days

one rotation
243 Earth days

moons
0

---

diameter
7,900 miles

distance from sun
93 million miles

one revolution
365 Earth days

one rotation
24 Earth hours

moons
1

---

diameter
4,200 miles

distance from sun
142 million miles

one revolution
687 Earth days

one rotation
25 Earth hours

moons
2

---

diameter
865,000 miles

The sun is a star.
Planets revolve
around it.

one rotation
27 Earth days

moons
0

This is an image of the surface of Venus measured by the Magellan probe. ▶

Image courtesy of NASA.

Mercury, Earth, and Mars rotate in the same direction as they orbit. Venus rotates in the opposite direction.

On Earth, one complete rotation occurs in about 24 hours. This is called a day. As the earth faces the sun, we have daytime. As it rotates away from the sun, we have nighttime. One Mercury day is about as long as 59 Earth days.

The length of time a planet takes to complete one revolution around the sun is called a year. For Earth, a year is about 365 days. On Mars, one year takes 687 Earth days. Mercury takes only 88 Earth days to complete a revolution.

Why does the moon seem to change shape?

You have learned that the sun has planets that revolve around it. Some planets have moons that revolve around them. The earth has one moon. Earth's moon completes one revolution around the earth about every 29 days. The moon completes a rotation on its axis in about the same amount of time.

Have you ever noticed how the moon looks different at certain times of the month? The moon goes through phases. A moon phase is the way the moon appears depending on how much of its sunlit surface is visible from the earth. We see different phases of the moon as the moon revolves around the earth.

Photos courtesy of NASA.

What are the phases of the moon?

The moon goes through eight named phases. This cycle follows the same pattern about every 29 days. This is how each moon phase looks from the earth.

1
new
moon

2
waxing
crescent

3
first
quarter

4
waxing
gibbous

5
full
moon

6
waning
gibbous

7
third
quarter

8
waning
crescent

Observing the moon

Write an answer for each of the following questions.

1. What will be the next moon phase after the waning crescent moon? _____

2. How does the appearance of the moon change over the course of a month? _____

_____

_____

_____

What are the five outer planets?

You have learned that there are nine planets in the solar system. The four inner planets are Mercury, Venus, Earth, and Mars. The five outer planets in order are Jupiter, Saturn, Uranus, Neptune, and Pluto.

Four of these outer planets are called "gas giants" because they are made from different types of gases. Pluto is not a gas planet.

Jupiter, Saturn, and Neptune all rotate in the same direction as their orbits, with the axis up and down. Uranus and Pluto rotate in the opposite direction.

Jupiter is the largest of all the planets. It rotates very quickly. Jupiter takes only ten hours to complete one rotation.

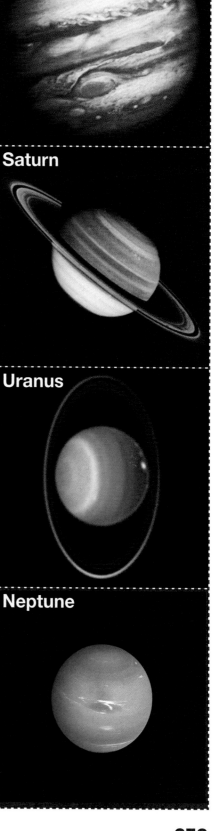

Jupiter

Saturn

Uranus

Pluto

Neptune

Photos courtesy of NASA.

diameter
89,000 miles

distance from sun
484 million miles

one revolution
12 Earth years

one rotation
10 Earth hours

moons
63

diameter
75,000 miles

distance from sun
886 million miles

one revolution
29 Earth years

one rotation
10 Earth hours

moons
50

diameter
32,000 miles

distance from sun
1,785 million miles

one revolution
84 Earth years

one rotation
17 Earth hours

moons
27

diameter
31,000 miles

distance from sun
2,800 million miles

one revolution
165 Earth years

one rotation
16 Earth hours

moons
13

diameter
1,400 miles

distance from sun
3,676 million miles

one revolution
248 Earth years

one rotation
6 Earth days

moons
1

Saturn has over 1,000 rings around it. Scientists have now learned that other planets have rings as well.

Uranus is unique. All the other planets rotate upright, like a spinning top. Uranus rolls like a ball on its side as it rotates.

Neptune is the most distant of the gas planets and is very difficult to study even with a powerful telescope. It appears to be blue in color.

Pluto is the smallest planet and is the farthest planet from the sun. It has never been explored by spacecraft from earth. Pluto is thought to be made of ice particles containing frozen methane gas and nitrogen.

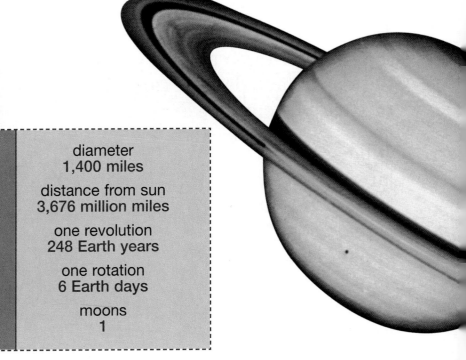

What do astronauts need?

Astronauts need oxygen to breathe, food to eat, and a place to sleep.

Oxygen tanks carry enough oxygen to help the astronauts breathe normally the entire trip.

Eating food can be a challenge for astronauts. Remember, there is no gravity in space, so things float freely. Imagine setting an apple on your plate and having it float away! You are also floating, so that makes it even more difficult. Astronauts have to anchor themselves down while they eat. There are no refrigerators on the shuttle, so the food is prepared so it can last up to six months. It is dehydrated, which means all the water has been taken out of it. When water is added back to the food, it becomes edible.

Astronaut Edward M. (Mike) Fincke, Expedition 9 NASA ISS science officer and flight engineer, floats fresh fruit inside the International Space Station.

Photos courtesy of NASA

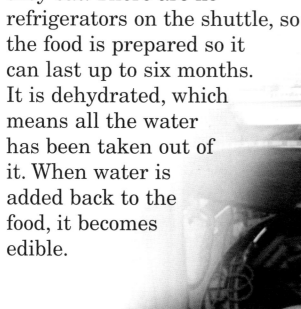

If eating is difficult, imagine trying to sleep! How do astronauts keep themselves in bed? They sleep in special compartments that are like large dressers so they do not have to worry about floating into something and hurting themselves.

Can you think of any more challenges that the astronauts face? How do you think astronauts handle them?

Astronaut Sandra H. Magnus, STS-112 mission specialist, washes her hair on the mid-deck of the Space Shuttle Atlantis.

Traveling Through Space

1. Name one challenge of space travel.

   _____

2. How do you think astronauts might handle this challenge?

   _____

   _____

3. What is one thing you would miss the most when traveling in space? Why?

   _____

   _____

What is the solar system?

Our solar system contains nine planets that revolve around the sun. Scientists have spent years collecting data using telescopes, probes, satellites, and manned space missions. Astronauts have faced many challenges when journeying into space to explore the unknown. Let's review what we have learned about space exploration.

Draw a line from the name to how it would best be used.

1. satellite   observing and doing experiments in space

2. astronaut   making objects far away appear closer

3. probe   relaying radio signals back to earth

4. telescope   exploring a very hot planet

NASA uses telescopes to view the earth from space.

Photo courtesy of NASA.

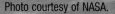

What are the names of the planets?

As you have explored our solar system, you have learned about the nine planets that revolve around the sun. Each planet takes a different amount of time to complete one revolution due to its distance from the sun. Some planets take less than one Earth year to complete one revolution, while other planets take hundreds of years.

Write the correct name next to each planet.

Photos and images courtesy of NASA.

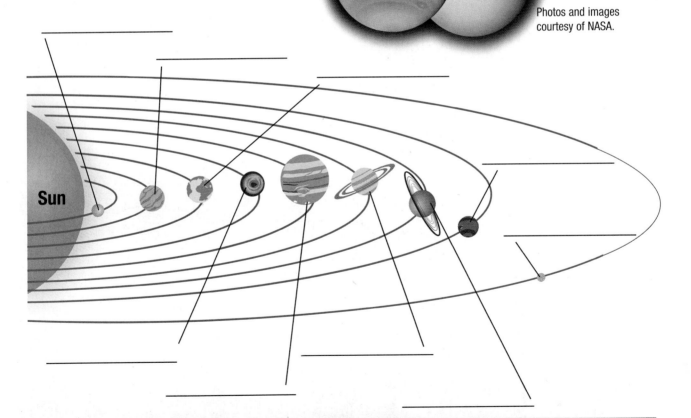

Sun

Word Bank
Mars Pluto Saturn Neptune Jupiter Earth Mercury Uranus Venus

Why does the moon seem to change shape?

The moon goes through a complete cycle of eight named phases about every 29 days. Look at the photos of each moon phase and answer the questions.

| 1 new moon | 2 waxing crescent | 3 first quarter | 4 waxing gibbous | 5 full moon | 6 waning gibbous | 7 third quarter | 8 waning crescent |

What will be the next moon phase after the first quarter?

_____

What was the moon phase before the waning crescent?

_____

What phase follows directly after a full moon?

_____

Why is it difficult to survive in space?

Study the photo. What dangers does this astronaut face? How is this space suit designed to protect an astronaut from those dangers?

_____

_____

_____

_____

_____

_____

Vocabulary Review

Use the Word Bank to complete each sentence.

Word Bank

solar system
moon phase
star
astronaut
orbit
probe
telescope
satellite
planet
axis

1. A _____ is a large body of rock or gas that orbits the sun.

2. An instrument that is used to observe faraway objects by making them appear larger and closer is a _____.

3. An _____ is a person who is trained to travel into space.

4. The imaginary line that goes through the middle of an object is an _____.

5. A glowing ball of burning gases is a _____.

6. Our _____ consists of nine planets, comets, asteroids, and moons that revolve around the sun.

7. An unmanned spacecraft sent into space to collect information is a _____.

8. The way the moon appears depending on how much of its sunlit surface is visible from the earth is called a _____.

9. A _____ is an object that revolves around a larger object in space.

10. An _____ is the path an object follows as it revolves around another object.

My Booklet about Stars and Constellations

Name _____

asteroid	gravity
astronomer	meteor
astronomy	meteorite
comet	meteoroid
constellation	star
galaxy	telescope

How do scientists study the universe?

When you look up into the night sky what do you think about? Have you ever tried to count the number of stars in the sky or wondered what else is out in space?

For centuries people have wondered the same thing. In fact, the night sky you look at hasn't changed much for thousands of years. How do we know this? We have records of people's observations, and we can calculate the changes in position of stars. Astronomy helps us to understand our universe. The study of the universe, including the solar system, stars, and galaxies is called **astronomy**. An **astronomer** is a scientist who studies the universe, including the sun, planets, and all the objects in space.

Photo courtesy of NASA, ESA and A. Nota (STScI/ESA)

Before the invention of the telescope, early astronomers used only their unaided eyes to observe space. They also used mathematics to help them determine speed and distance of objects in space. Nicolas Copernicus determined through observations and calculations that the earth moved around the sun. His discovery was made sometime between 1508 and 1514.

After the invention of the telescope, Galileo was able to observe the surface of our moon. In January, 1610, he also discovered that Jupiter has four moons revolving around it. A telescope is an instrument that is used to observe faraway objects by making them appear larger and closer.

The telescope opened the door for other great astronomers. In 1912, Henrietta Leavitt discovered what causes stars to be so bright and Edwin Hubble observed distant galaxies. Hubble began classifying the shapes of galaxies in 1926.

Henrietta Leavitt
The American Association of Variable Star Observers (AAVSO), Cambridge, MA

As technology improves and scientists invent newer observational tools and more powerful computers, the capacity for observation and calculation increases. Powerful telescopes allow scientists to see into deep space. Some telescopes are located on mountaintops or in remote areas far away from bright city lights. Two of the world's largest telescopes are the Keck Telescopes located on Mauna Kea in Hawaii.

At the summit of Mauna Kea, Hawaii, NASA astronomers have linked the two telescopes at the W. M. Keck Observatory. This is the world's most powerful optical telescope system.
Photo courtesy of NASA.

Astronomers use photography, radar, radio signals, and other instruments to explore the vast darkness of space. They have discovered the three planets beyond Saturn—Uranus, Neptune, and Pluto—along with other distant galaxies. They have also identified over 50,000 asteroids revolving around the sun. In this chapter you will learn some of the amazing things that astronomers have discovered about the universe that God created.

The Hubble Space Telescope orbits the earth about every 97 minutes.

Photo courtesy of NASA.

Learning About Astronomy

Fill in the circle next to the correct word to complete each sentence.

1. Astronomy is the study of the _____.

    ○ rocks   ○ ocean   ○ universe

2. Astronomers have discovered new _____.

    ○ planets   ○ chemicals   ○ landforms

3. A telescope is an instrument used to observe objects that are _____.

    ○ close up   ○ far away   ○ microscopic

This photo was taken by the Hubble Space Telescope as it looked into deep space.

Photo courtesy of NASA and The Hubble Heritage Team (AURA/STScI)

What is a shooting star?

Astronomers have observed many bright objects in space including asteroids, comets, and meteors. But what are the differences between them?

An asteroid is a chunk of rock and metal that orbits the sun. Asteroids can vary in size and shape. Most asteroids orbit the sun in an area called the asteroid belt, which is located between Mars and Jupiter.

A comet is a frozen chunk of ice, dust, and rock that orbits the sun. Comets are often called "dirty snowballs" because of the way they look. A comet contains three parts: the nucleus, coma, and tail. As the comet nears the sun, the nucleus begins to melt and the ice turns into gases. The gases that form a ball around the nucleus of the comet are called the coma. As solar winds blow across the coma, a tail is formed behind the nucleus and coma.

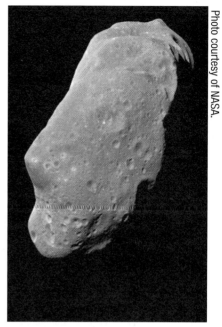

▲ Asteroid Ida

▲ Comet Hale-Bopp

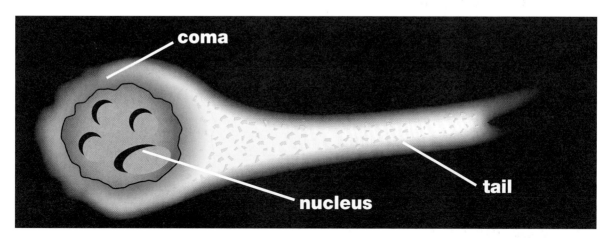

A meteoroid is a small rock fragment from an asteroid or comet. Meteoroids are located in space outside the earth's atmosphere. When a meteoroid enters the earth's atmosphere and burns up it is called a meteor. As the meteor is burning, a bright streak of light is visible in the sky. A meteoroid that does not burn up completely and that lands on the earth's surface is called a meteorite. A crater is formed when a meteorite hits the surface.

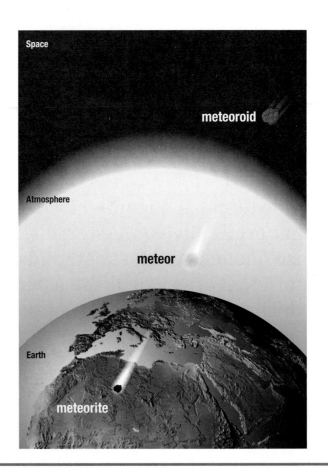

Exploring Objects in the Sky

Use the Word Bank to complete each sentence. One word will not be used.

Word Bank
meteor
ice
asteroid
comet
crater
meteoroid

1. When a meteorite hits the surface of the earth it forms a _____.

2. A _____ is a meteoroid that enters the earth's atmosphere and burns up.

3. A _____ has a nucleus, coma, and tail.

4. A comet is a frozen chunk of _____, dust, and rock.

5. An _____ is a chunk of rock and metal.

This close-up photo of an exploded star was taken by the Hubble Space Telescope.

Photo courtesy of NASA

What is a star?

What shape do you usually think of when you think of a star? Most people probably think of a five-pointed twinkling star, but stars are actually round!

A star is a glowing ball of burning gases. There are billions of stars in our solar system, but only about 6,000 are visible without the use of a telescope. Stars are always in the sky, but they cannot be seen during the day because the sun's bright light is scattered in the atmosphere.

Stars come in a wide range of sizes. The sun measures about 432,000 miles (695,500 kilometers) from its center to its surface. However, astronomers classify the sun as a dwarf star! The largest stars are called supergiants. Some supergiants can be 1,000 times as large as the sun. The smallest stars are neutron stars. Neutron stars can be as small as 6 miles (10 kilometers) from center to surface.

Astronomers also classify stars according to color. The color of a star shows its surface temperature. Blue stars are the hottest, followed by white, yellow, orange, and red. The sun is a yellow star.

Some familiar stars are the North Star (Polaris), Sirius, and Alpha Centauri. The North Star is used as a directional tool, Sirius is the brightest nighttime star, and Alpha Centauri is the second closest star to the earth.

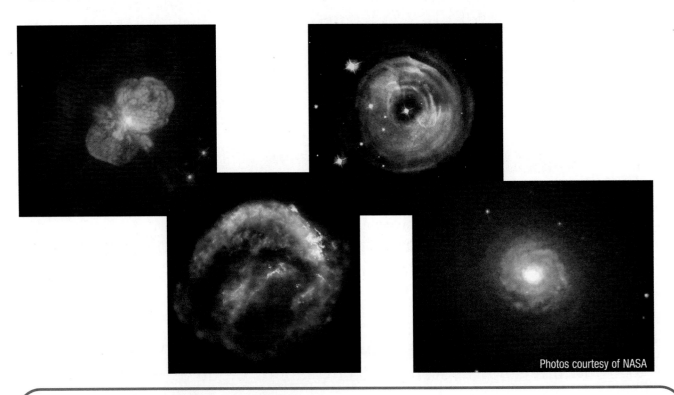

Photos courtesy of NASA

Understanding Stars

Draw a line to match the type of star with its description.

1. Blue supergiant   a cool, small star

2. Red dwarf   a hot, small star

3. Yellow dwarf   a very hot, large star

4. Red giant   a cool, large star

elliptical galaxy

spiral galaxy

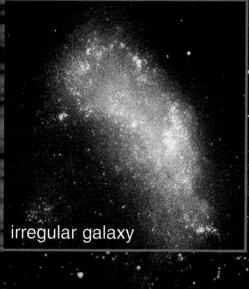
irregular galaxy

What is the Milky Way?

You have learned that all the planets, the sun, and other nearby objects in space are part of a solar system. Our solar system belongs to a galaxy called the Milky Way.

A galaxy is a huge collection of stars, gases, and dust clouds that are found in space. This collection of objects moves around the center of the galaxy and is held together by a force called gravity. Gravity is the force pulling together all objects in the universe.

◀ The Milky Way as seen from Earth.

Astronomers have classified galaxies into three main types according to their shapes. The three types are elliptical, spiral, and irregular.

An elliptical galaxy looks like a flattened ball. It is the most common type of galaxy and can be very large.

A spiral galaxy looks like a pinwheel. It has arms that branch out from the center and turn. Our galaxy, the Milky Way, is a spiral galaxy. We see it from the edge, so it looks like a milky band in the night sky.

An irregular galaxy has no special shape. It is smaller and less common. The two galaxies closest to us are irregular galaxies called the Magellanic Clouds.

Learning About Galaxies

Draw a line from the picture of the galaxy to its description.

An irregular galaxy has no special shape.

An elliptical galaxy is shaped like a flattened ball.

A spiral galaxy is shaped like a pinwheel with long arms that turn.

What is a constellation?

For thousands of years, people have observed that stars appear in patterns that remind them of familiar things. They gave these star patterns names like Bull and Bear. These patterns are called constellations.

A constellation is a group of stars that forms a pattern in the shape of an animal, person, or object and is named for that shape. Currently, there are 88 named constellations. People have invented the names and stories that go with each constellation.

Did you know?

Did you know that the Bible also refers to constellations in the sky? Imagine, the stars you are looking at are the very same stars that Jesus saw when He was on this earth!

The North Star is part of the constellation called the Little Dipper. It is also called Ursa Minor, the Little Bear. You have to use your imagination to connect the stars and then fill in the picture of the dipper or the bear. The Big Dipper or Ursa Major, the Great Bear is located very close to the Little Dipper.

Naming the Constellations

Connect the numbered stars to make a constellation. Write the name of the constellation on the blank.

This is a picture of the night sky above Hohenzollern Castle, Southern Germany. The stars have been enhanced by a broadening filter (for a better identification of the constellation

Till Credner, AlltheSky.com

Constellation name: _____

How are stars and constellations used?

Before the invention of clocks and calendars, people would use the sun, stars, and constellations to tell time. The stars in constellations move with the seasons. Farmers would study the stars to help them determine when to plant their crops.

Stars and constellations were also used as navigational tools. When you are facing the North Star, you are facing north. This means that east will be on your right-hand side and west on your left-hand side. That means that south would be which direction?

Farmers can use the movement of the stars and constellations to determine when to plant their crops.

Sailors would use the location of certain stars and constellations to help guide their ships at sea. They used compasses to keep their ships on course.

Using Stars and Constellations

1. If you were lost in the woods at night, how would you use the stars to help you get back to camp?

_____

_____

_____

2. If you were facing the North Star, which direction would west be?

_____

_____

_____

3. Why would a farmer need to know when a new season begins?

_____

_____

_____

What do we know about objects in space?

Astronomy is the study of the universe, including the sun, planets, and all the other objects in space. What are some of the space objects that you have observed in this chapter?

Photo courtesy of NASA.

Write **True** or **False** next to each sentence.

1. _____ An astronomer uses a telescope to observe faraway objects by making them appear larger and closer.

2. _____ Galileo used a telescope to observe Jupiter.

3. _____ Astronomers never use math to help them calculate the distance of objects.

What is a meteor?

Meteoroids, small rock fragments from an asteroid or comet, are classified according to their relation to the earth's surface. Label the drawing using the following words: **meteor**, **meteoroid**, and **meteorite**.

_____

_____

_____

Draw a line from the name of the object to its definition.

1. comet

2. meteorite

3. asteroid

• a chunk of rock and metal that orbits the sun

• a frozen chunk of ice, dust, and rock that orbits the sun

• a meteoroid that does not burn up completely and that lands on the earth's surface

What is the Milky Way galaxy?

A galaxy is a huge collection of stars, gases, and dust clouds. Scientists classify galaxies according to shape. Do you remember the shapes? Fill in the circle next to the correct answer.

1. An elliptical galaxy is shaped like a flattened _____.
   ○ ball   ○ shoe   ○ box

2. A spiral galaxy, when viewed from the top looks like a ___ .
   ○ jar   ○ marble   ○ pinwheel

3. An _____ galaxy has no special shape.
   ○ elliptical   ○ irregular   ○ spiral

What is that constellation?

A group of stars that forms a picture of an animal, person, or object is called a constellation. There are currently 88 constellations. Some constellations can only be seen in certain parts of the world. Name this constellation.

Till Credner, AlltheSky.com

Vocabulary Review

Use the Word Bank to complete each sentence. Some words will not be used.

1. A glowing ball of burning gases is a
_____.

2. The force pulling together all objects in the universe is called _____.

3. An instrument that is used to observe faraway objects by making them appear larger and closer is a _____.

4. An _____ is a person who studies the universe, including the sun, planets, and all the other objects in space.

5. A _____ is a group of stars that forms a pattern in the shape of an animal, person, or object and is named after that shape.

6. A frozen chunk of ice, dust, and rock that orbits the sun is called a _____.

7. The study of the universe, including the solar system, stars, and galaxies is called _____.

8. A huge collection of stars, gases, and dust clouds is called a _____.

A

active volcano A volcano that continues to erupt. (page 249)

adaptation A way that animals adjust to changes in their environment. (page 13)

angular motion The motion of an object around a central point. (page 87)

asteroid A chunk of rock and metal that orbits the sun. (page 287)

astronaut A person who is trained to travel into space. (page 265)

astronomer A scientist who studies the universe, including the sun, planets, and all other objects in space. (page 283)

astronomy The study of the universe, including the solar system, stars, and galaxies. (page 283)

atom The basic component of matter. (page 63)

attract To pull towards. (page 105)

autonomic nervous system A system that controls all involuntary actions of the body. (page 173)

avalanche A large amount of snow that slides down the side of a mountain. (page 247)

axis An imaginary line that goes through the middle of an object. (page 269)

B

ball-and-socket joint A joint that allows movement in all directions. (page 150)

bone marrow A jelly-like material that makes blood cells and is located within the spaces of the spongy bone. (page 147)

botanist A scientist who studies plants. (page 25)

botany The study of plants. (page 25)

brain stem The part of the brain that connects the brain to the spinal cord. It controls involuntary muscles that work to keep your body alive. (page 170)

bulb A kind of underground stem. (page 48)

 C

camouflage The way an organism blends in with its environment. (page 14)

canyon A valley that is very deep and has steep, rocky cliffs. (page 230)

carbohydrate The nutrient that provides the biggest energy source for the body. Examples include pasta, breads and cereals, potatoes, and fruits. (page 188)

carbon dioxide A colorless, odorless gas that people and animals breathe out of their lungs. Plants use it to make food. (page 27)

cardiac muscle A type of muscle found only in the heart. (page 153)

cartographer A person who makes maps. (page 245)

cell membrane The thin covering of a cell. (page 29)

cell wall The stiff layer outside the cell membrane of the plant cell. (page 29)

cerebellum The part of the brain that is located below the cerebrum. It controls balance, movement, and coordination. (page 170)

cerebrum The largest part of the brain. It controls thinking and voluntary movements. (page 169)

chemical reaction The rearrangement of atoms within molecules to make new molecules with different properties. (page 75)

chemist A scientist who studies the properties of matter. (page 65)

chlorophyll The green coloring in a plant that captures the sun's energy. (page 28)

chloroplast The tiny green part inside a plant cell. (page 29)

circuit A path that electricity can flow through. (page 109)

classify To put similar things in the same group. (page 55)

coastline The place where the land meets the ocean. (page 235)

comet A frozen chunk of ice, dust, and rock that orbits the sun. (page 287)

compact bone The smooth, hard, white layer of bone. (page 147)

compete When one organism works against another to get what it needs to survive. (page 11)

compound machine A combination of two or more simple machines. (page 96)

conductor Material that allows electricity to easily flow through it. (page 108)

conservation of matter The principle that states that matter can change form, but it cannot be created or destroyed. (page 69)

constellation A group of stars that forms a pattern in the shape of an animal, person, or object and is named for that shape. (page 293)

consumer An organism that eats food. (page 7)

continent One of the earth's seven major land masses. (page 223)

cycle of matter The process of matter undergoing a change and eventually going back to its original form. (page 70)

cytoplasm The jelly-like material that fills the inside of a plant cell. (page 29)

 D

decomposer An organism that breaks down dead plant and animal material to return it to the soil. (page 7)

deposition The process by which a gas directly becomes a solid. (page 72)

diet All the food a person eats, whether healthy or unhealthy. (page 191)

dormant volcano A volcano that has not erupted in recent years. (page 249)

 E

earthquake The shaking of the earth's surface that is caused by the sudden movement of the earth's crust. (page 251)

ecologist A scientist who studies the relationship between living things and their environment. (page 4)

ecology The scientific study of the relationships between living things and their environments. (page 4)

ecosystem A group of living and nonliving things that interact with each other in an environment. (page 4)

electric current The flow of electricity through a conductor. (page 109)

electric discharge The flow of electric charges through the air from one object to another. (page 107)

electrical engineer A person who designs new technology that uses electrical energy. (page 106)

electricity The flow of charged particles. (page 104)

electromagnet A magnet made from a piece of iron wrapped with a coil of wire through which an electric current is moving. (page 130)

elevation How high land rises above sea level. (page 227)

environment Everything around an organism. (page 3)

erosion The removal of rock and soil by wind and water. (pages 230, 244)

F

fat The nutrient that provides a concentrated energy source for the body. Examples include eggs, dairy products, meats, avocados, some nuts, and oils. (page 188)

fault A crack in the earth's crust. (page 251)

food chain The way food passes from one organism to another. (page 8)

food web Several food chains that are connected. (page 8)

force The push or pull of one object on another object. (page 89)

friction The force that resists motion of one object against another. (page 89)

 G

galaxy A huge collection of stars, gases, and dust clouds. (page 291)

gas Matter whose molecules move so fast that they fly away from one another in random directions. (page 71)

geographer A scientist who studies the earth's surface. (page 225)

geologist A scientist who studies the earth. (page 203)

germinate When a seed begins to grow. (page 33)

gravity The force pulling together all objects in the universe. (pages 90, 291)

 H

habit Something that you do so often that it becomes a regular part of your life. (page 195)

heredity The passing of characteristics from parent to offspring. (page 35)

hibernate To rest through the cold winter. (page 13)

hinge joint A joint that moves back and forth like the hinges on a door. (page 149)

humus The decaying plant and animal matter in soil that helps plants grow. (page 213)

hybrid A plant that has parents of different varieties, or kinds. (page 36)

igneous rock Rock that is formed when magma or lava cools and hardens. (page 209)

insulator Material that does not allow electricity to flow through it easily. (page 108)

involuntary movement A movement that you do not consciously control. (page 153)

joint The connection between two bones. (page 149)

lake A large body of water surrounded by land. (page 233)

landform A feature of the earth's surface. (pages 223, 243)

landslide A large amount of dry soil and rock that slides down a steep slope. (page 247)

left hemisphere The part of the brain that usually controls the right side of the body. (page 171)

ligament A tough band of tissue that connects bone to bone. (page 149)

linear motion The motion of an object along a straight line. (page 84)

lines of force The invisible lines connecting the north and south poles of a magnet. (page 131)

liquid Matter whose molecules are packed close together, but the molecules in liquids move fast enough to have some freedom and not be confined to certain positions. (page 71)

magnet A metallic object that attracts other objects made of iron, steel, or certain other metals. (page 125)

magnetic field The space surrounding a magnet in which the magnet's force is active. (page 131)

magnetic pole A place on a magnet where its magnetic force is strongest. (page 127)

magnetism An invisible force that attracts objects made of iron or related metals. (page 125)

mass The amount of matter in an object. (page 63)

matter Anything that occupies space and that we can see, smell, taste, hear, and touch. (page 63)

measurement system A collection of specific standards that a group of people agree to use for measuring things. (page 67)

metamorphic rock Rock that is formed when heat and pressure are applied to igneous or sedimentary rock. (page 210)

meteor A meteoroid that enters the earth's atmosphere and burns up. (page 288)

meteorite A meteoroid that does not burn up completely and that lands on the earth's surface. (page 288)

meteoroid A small rock fragment from an asteroid or comet. (page 288)

metric system A measurement system that uses the meter as the standard of length. (page 67)

microscope An instrument that uses lenses and light to make it easier for people to see small objects. (page 29)

microscopic Describes something that is too small to be seen without the use of a microscope. (page 29)

migrate To move from one place to another. (page 13)

mineral A non-living, natural substance found in the earth. (page 207) In foods, a mineral helps keep the body healthy and working properly. Examples include iron, calcium, potassium, and zinc. (page 189)

mixture Any combination of substances that can be physically separated. (page 73)

molecule Two or more atoms connected together. (page 63)

moon phase The way the moon appears depending on how much of its sunlit surface is visible from the earth. (page 271)

motion The change in an object's location over a certain amount of time. (page 83)

motor nerve A type of nerve that carries information from the brain to other body parts. (page 167)

mountain A landform that usually rises at least 2,000 feet (610 m) above the earth's surface. (page 227)

mudslide A large amount of wet soil and rock that slides down a steep slope. (page 248)

neurologist A doctor who treats disorders of the nervous system. (page 164)

niche A special role or job. (page 12)

nucleus The control center of the cell. (page 29)

nutrient A substance in food that keeps the body working properly. The six nutrients the body needs are water, carbohydrates, proteins, fats, vitamins, and minerals. (page 187)

nutritionist A person who evaluates people's health and recommends special diet plans to help them get or stay healthy. (page 186)

orbit The path an object follows as it revolves around another object. (page 267)

organism Any living thing. (page 3)

oxygen A colorless, odorless gas in the air that is needed for most living things to stay alive. (page 27)

 P

parallel circuit A circuit that allows more than one path for electricity to flow through. (page 111)

periodic motion The back-and-forth motion of an object from a central point. (page 88)

perish To die. (page 15)

petals The outside parts of a flower that attract a pollinator to the flower. (page 31)

phloem The stem tissue that moves food, made by photosynthesis in the leaves, to the rest of the plant. (page 47)

photosynthesis The process that allows green plants to make food from water, carbon dioxide, and sunlight. (page 28)

physicist A scientist who studies motion. (page 86)

pistil The part in a flower where seeds are formed. (page 31)

pivot joint A joint that allows bones to turn. (page 149)

plain A mostly flat, level area of land. (page 231)

planet A large body of rock or gas that revolves around the sun. (page 267)

plant biologist A scientist who studies how plants live and function in their environment. (page 45)

plant cutting The parts of a plant such as a leaf, stem, or root that can grow to make another plant. (page 34)

plant division The process of splitting apart a plant to produce new plants. (page 34)

plant propagation The process of using a part of a plant to increase the number of that plant. (page 33)

pollen A fine powder in a flower that is needed to make seeds. (page 31)

pollination The process by which pollen is carried to the pistil of a flower. (pages 32, 51)

pollinator The insect or animal that carries the pollen to the pistil. (pages 31, 51)

power The amount of work done over a certain amount of time. (page 91)

predator An animal that hunts another animal for food. (page 9)

prey An animal that is hunted by a predator. (page 9)

probe An unmanned spacecraft that is sent into space to collect information. (page 264)

producer An organism that can make its own food. (page 7)

properties The unique characteristics of matter. (page 63)

prosthesis An artificial body part. (page 155)

protein The nutrient that helps repair and build body tissues. Examples include dairy products, meats, beans, nuts, and whole grains. (page 188)

pure substance Matter that contains only one kind of substance. (page 73)

radiologist A doctor who looks at x-rays and finds ways to help people get better. (page 146)

relocate To move to a new location to live. (page 15)

repel To push away. (pages 105, 127)

resistor A material that slows down, but does not stop, an electric current. (page 113)

revolution The movement of one object completely around another object. (page 267)

right hemisphere The part of the brain that usually

controls the left side of the body. (page 171)

river A body of freshwater that flows from an upland source to a large lake or to the sea. (page 233)

rock cycle The process through which rocks change from one form to another. (page 211)

root The part of a plant that holds it in the ground and absorbs water and nutrients. (page 47)

rotation The spinning of an object on its axis. (page 269)

rotational motion The motion of an object in a complete circle. (page 87)

S

satellite An object that revolves around a larger object in space. (page 264)

scavenger An animal that eats dead animals. (page 10)

scientific classification A system for sorting similar organisms into named groups in order to help scientists communicate quickly and easily. (page 55)

sedimentary rock Rock that is formed when layers of minerals pile up, stick to each other, and harden. (page 209)

sensory nerve A type of nerve that carries information from the body parts to the brain. (page 167)

series circuit A circuit that allows only one path for electricity to flow through. (page 111)

simple machine A tool that requires only one force to be used. (page 95)

simple plants A group of plants that do not flower or produce seeds. (page 53)

skeletal muscle A type of muscle attached to bones. It produces voluntary movements. (page 151)

smooth muscle A type of muscle found in the stomach and intestines. (page 153)

soil The loose material that covers the surface of the earth and supports plant growth. It is made of tiny pieces of rocks and minerals, humus, water, and air. (page 213)

solar system The sun and all the objects that revolve around it. (page 267)

solid Matter whose molecules are packed close together and can barely move. (page 71)

solution A mixture that acts like a pure substance. (page 73)

spongy bone A type of bone that looks like a sponge and is found deeper inside the bone. (page 147)

spore A microscopic single cell that does not need to be pollinated to become a new plant. (page 53)

stamen The part of the flower that produces pollen. (page 31)

star A glowing ball of burning gases. (pages 268, 289)

state of matter The physical property that defines how molecules are arranged in the matter. (page 71)

static electricity The sudden flow of charged particles from the buildup of electric charges on the surface of an object. (page 105)

stem The part of a plant that supports the leaves, flowers, and seeds and moves water, nutrients, and food to the rest of the plant. (page 47)

sublimation The process by which a solid becomes a gas. (page 72)

substance Matter with a unique arrangement of atoms that makes it different from other kinds of matter. (page 73)

switch A device that can open or close a circuit. (page 110)

telescope An instrument that is used to observe faraway objects by making them appear larger and closer. (pages 263, 284)

tendon A strong, connective tissue that binds muscles to bones. (page 151)

tsunami A series of large ocean waves caused by an underwater earthquake or volcanic eruption. (page 253)

tuber A kind of underground stem. (page 48)

valley An area of low-lying land surrounded by higher ground. (page 229)

velocity The distance that an object travels over a certain amount of time. (page 85)

vitamin A substance in food that helps keep the body healthy and working properly. Examples include A, B, C, D, E, and K. (page 189)

volcano An opening in the earth's crust that spews out lava, hot ash, and gases during an eruption. (page 249)

voluntary movement A movement a person can control. (page 151)

work Using force on an object to make it move. (page 91)

xylem The stem tissue that moves water and nutrients from the roots to the rest of the plant. (page 47)